From The Diary of an Assassin

From The Diary of an Assassin

INTRODUCING || ANGEL - A HUSTLING DIVA WITH A TWIST

Brenda Wright

Brenda Wright

CONTENTS

Acknowledgment

I want to express my gratitude to everyone who reads my book and accompanies me on this journey. I wish to convey my gratefulness to my husband (William) for always having my back with his financial help and support. I want to express my gratitude to my three granddaughters (Jasmine, Keiasia, and Sharaine) for their help in sending e-mails. I want to express my appreciation to my two grandsons (Kaylen and Keith). Also, I'd like to thank all my family members and friends for being there for me, lending a listening ear, and providing constructive feedback. We appreciate your support throughout my journey. I'll do my best not to disappoint anyone. You all have a special place in my heart. I'd also like to express my gratitude to Icon Works Media and its staff for assisting me in publishing my book.

So much love,
Brenda G. Wright

First Printing, 2012

Library of Congress Control Number: 2012904965
ISBN: Softcover   979-8-9850921-0-3
         E-book   979-8-9850921-2-7

This book is a work of fiction. Names, characters, places, and incidents are either the product of the author's imagination or used fictitiously. Any resemblance to any actual persons, living or dead, events, or locales is entirely coincidental.

One

The Beginning of Angel: A Hustling Diva-turned-assassin

Angel was born and raised in the lower Westside of Chicago to a crack-head mother named Gloria Black. Gloria, known by the nickname Glow, was the neighborhood slut who made sex with every man in the hood to keep her habit going. Glow was a pretty black woman with a caramel complexion with silky long black hair, weighed one hundred and thirty pounds, and stood five feet six.

One day, while she was going into a crack house, Glow met a guy who took an immediate interest in her looks and saw her potential. She was a crackhead, but she kept her appearance up. Everyone in the hood knew what Glow was about, and they also knew the Hawaiian kingpin named Cane, a mobster who ran both the Westside and the Southside. He had an entire army of soldiers under his wing. He didn't take any shorts with his money. Cane was a very handsome man with dark skin, slender, had swagger worse than Denzel, and always dressed to suit his kingpin status. He also owned a club that he called club sexy, where he had strippers dancing on poles. It has a gambling room in the back and a dope room on the second floor. Cane doesn't sell ounces. So if you wanted to purchase some weight, Cane was the man.

Cane couldn't get this beautiful crackhead woman he saw two days ago out of his mind. He wanted to go back in the hood to see if she was still there. Still, he decided against it because he didn't roll like that. So instead, came up with the idea to send his right-hand man to the crack house.

Cane wanted to see if Glow was hanging out there. But, to his dismay, she had been there all night. He didn't want her to find out that his soldiers were watching out for her. But there was something about this woman that kept his mind on lock. He couldn't shake the feeling she had in him. No woman had that kind of power over Cane, the kingpin. So he knew he had to find out who she was and how she got in that predicament.

Cane knew she was going to be his as soon as he could pinpoint her problems. One day he received a call stating that Glow was at the crack house having a seizure, and they were getting ready to call an ambulance. He told the caller not to call an ambulance, and he would send someone to pick her up and bring her to him. Instead, he instructed the caller to make sure she didn't bite her tongue and keep her comfortable until her ride gets there.

Glow was unconscious when Cane's right-hand man picks her up. The sight of her made Cane sweat, and he admired her beauty. He wanted nothing more but for her to be healthy and safe. The following day, when Glow woke up, she didn't recognize the place and why she was there.

Glow realized she was in a place that was so beautiful. She knew thought it was a dream. She only saw houses like that in magazines. Glow recognized the handsome man in front of her, but what she didn't understand was why he was there. She soon found out that she held the key to Cane kingpin's heart.

Cane kept her in a room with a doctor to help her kick her cocaine habit. It was the longest two weeks of her life. But when she had finally kicked her addiction, she knew Cane wanted something in return.

Cane had his maid fix breakfast for Glow. After eating breakfast, Cane asked her to meet him out on the terrace, and she did. Then Cane told Glow he wanted nothing in return. He just wanted to be her man if she would have him.

Glow remembered how she grew up poor and how she got molested all the time by her mother's boyfriends and close relatives in her father's family. So what else could she possibly lose? So she decided that if he wanted to have a place in her life, she wanted everything that money could buy.

She became the queen bee of all Cane's crack houses, and club sexy became her number one spot. Cane took Glow on shopping trips to New York, Las Vegas, Paris, and France. She spent money like she was born wealthy. He was happy to spoil Glow. She meant the world to him, and he knew one day she would rule his castle.

Cane wanted Glow to shine, so he took her to Tiffanies. He iced out Glow's body with white diamonds from head to toe. Cane wished to have a party. Reintroduce her to the people in the hood who knew her as Glow, the crackhead. So he draped her in a five thousand dollar Donna Karan dress and three thousand dollar Donna Karan stilettos and the bag to match.

When she stepped out of her dressing room, she was in a cloud. Her man Cane had on a royal blue Donna Karan suit to match her dress. He had on some royal blue Donna Karan snakeskin banisters. They both were a force to be reckoned with. Cane went all out for the woman he's going to marry.

Cane and Glow had been going hot and heavy for two years. They even bought another house with five bedrooms, five bathrooms, and three-car garages for a Rose Royce, Jaguar, and a Hummer. A beautiful kitchen with stainless steel appliances, decorated with beautiful marble floors, and furniture designed by Donna Karan. She also decorated each room with precise detail. Cane made sure the house was picture book perfect. The house ranked number one in the weekly magazine.

Cane and Glow were hot and heavy in sex. Glow even missed her period for three months, and she didn't even notice. She was so happy until one morning they were having breakfast when Cane looked at her rear end and saw she had more junk in her trunk, and they laughed.

Glow didn't do things as most women do. She didn't have morning sickness at all, but her breast and butt pick up a little weight. So, Glow decided that morning, she would pay the doctor's office a visit as a walk-in because she couldn't wait. She wanted to know as soon as possible. So Glow finished her breakfast, took a quick shower, and headed out for the doctor's office.

Glow did the usual tests, and to her surprise, she was three months pregnant. She was happy but scared, not because she was with a baby. But because of being pregnant by a Hawaiian kingpin who kills at the drop of a hat.

Glow knew in her heart that Cane loved her, and their child would have everything that they wanted. When Glow finally made it home from the doctor's office, Cane was sitting in his office, waiting to hear the good news. He knew he didn't shoot blanks.

Cane also knew that he had to make dinner arrangements for his marriage proposal. He had to make sure everything was right. The ring that he purchased for Glow was a twenty thousand dollar platinum ten-carat pink diamond engagement ring. He had the Terrence decked out like they were in Hawaii, the palm trees were beautiful, and the dinner menu was off the chain.

The chef prepared lobster, crab salad, steamed vegetables, and buttered breadsticks for dessert. They had chocolate mousse; the music playing softly in the background was one of Teddy Pendergrass's songs. She didn't even think a man of his caliber had it going on like that.

The lights were dim, and he took her hand into his and gazed into her eyes. He asked her would she be his wife. She said yes without a second thought; she wanted to marry this man. Glow fell in love with Cane in only six months. She didn't even know his actual legal name. She was about to ask him when he reached his hand out to introduce himself to her as Clarence Cantrell carter. A.K.A. Cane. Six months later, their little bundle of joy was born. Seven pounds and six ounces. She was born with black curly hair and big hazel brown eyes. The most beautiful baby Glow had ever seen. Cane and Glow agreed to name her Angel Candice Carter. A.K.A., Baby Girl, born to Clarence and Gloria Carter. Soon to be the hustling diva with a twist!

After Angel was born, Cane started taking long trips to California for business meetings without Glow. She never questions what he was doing out of town because she trusted her man. Until one day, in particular, he came home suddenly. The phone rang. When she answered, the caller on the other end hangs up. Glow just chopped it up as someone playing on the phone.

Cane went straight into his daughter's room, watched her sleep. His baby girl was as beautiful as her mother. He had made plans to take his wife out for dinner that night. He wanted to tell her about another business trip and will be away for two weeks this time.

Cane didn't know how she would handle it, so he had to set the stage upright because he learned one thing about Glow. She didn't play with her man. When he told Glow what his plans were, she felt a bad feeling in her stomach, so she asked Cane was he taking any of his soldiers with him. He told her no, he could handle his business on his own. That situation didn't sit right with Glow, but she had to trust her man.

Two days later, Cane was packing for his two-week trip, and glow still harvested the same funny feeling she had the night cane told her about his journey. She said nothing because she wasn't about to spoil her man trip.

She started getting those phone calls again, with the phone ringing all times of night with no one on the other end. So she would take the phone off the hook at night to get a peaceful night's sleep while her baby girl was asleep.

Cane would call her every night at seven, so she felt safe taking the phone off the hook at night. One night a dream had awakened her out of her sleep about Cane. He was in trouble. She could feel the pain he was in, and it frightens her so severely she broke out in a sweat.

Glow put the phone back on the hook to call Cane. But when she called his hotel room, she didn't get an answer. That really frightens her, so she called the hotel front desk, and to her dismay, Cane didn't even have a room at the hotel. He told her he would stay in. That really made

Glow get out of bed and make some calls to Cane's soldiers and his right-hand man.

She knew if anyone knew what was going on, his right-hand man Silk knew. So Glow called Silk, and he answered on the first ring. She asked Silk if he had heard anything from Cane. He told her he had spoken to Cane that morning and everything was alright with him.

Glow didn't believe Silk because her feelings were telling her something different. So she decided she had to do a brief investigation on her own. Still, before she could get dressed, the doorbell rang, and the UPS man was standing there with a box waiting for her signature.

When she opened the box, Glow screamed out loud and almost passed out when she saw what was in the box. Inside the box was Cane's head. She cried so loud until she woke up their baby girl.

She had to pull herself and call Silk to tell her what the hell was going on and who was with Cane, that they wanted his head on a silver platter. Glow is concerned because she couldn't have a proper funeral for Cane without a body.

Glow had a memorial for Cane, but she wasn't giving up on him. Someone had to tell her what happened to her husband. Silk always had a secret crush on Glow, but he wasn't about to cross Cane while he was still alive, anyway.

She couldn't pull herself together without Cane. He saved Glow from a life of destruction, pain, and suffering. Glow didn't think she could be on her own without the man who pulled her out of the gutter.

Silk knew she needed Cane, and he knew without him, he could slide in and make things better for Glow. But Silk didn't realize that Glow suspects it involved him for what happened to Cane. So she will never trust him. Glow didn't know Cane left her wealthy for the rest of her life, and Silk knew this. That's why he had a part in what happened to cane with the Italian mafia.

Two

~

Cane's Double Life

Cane was leading a double life that Glow was unaware of. When he met Glow, he had already married a black woman of Italian origin named Rakia Salvador. Mr. Salvador, the head of the Italian mafia, is Rakia's father. Cane was his employee. That's how Cane got his start in life. When he met Rakia, he had nothing.

He moved to Chicago to take over one of the family businesses, unaware that he was being watched the entire time. Cane and Rakia had two sons together, who are prepared to join the family business when they turn twenty-one.

Don, Cane's father-in-law's right-hand man, sent Mr. Salvador information about Cane and Glow's wedding and the birth of their daughter. Mr. Salvador was enraged by the news, and that Cane could treat Rakia like trash irritated him; Cane had to pay for his mistakes. So he called Cane on his personal phone and demanded that he spend some time with the family.

Cane did what his father-in-law told him to do because he understood what Mr. Salvador was all about. He knew he couldn't risk anything because he had another family to protect. So Cane arrived in Hawaii on time. He was there three days before the shitstorm.

Mr. Salvador wanted to discuss some family business with Cane while they were all eating dinner. So they went to Mr. Salvador's office, as usual, with four of his bodyguards close behind. Mr. Salvador reached into his cigar box, lit it, and took a long drag.

Mr. Salvador reached across his desk for an envelope left for him by Don. Cane's face turned blue when Mr. Salvador opened it and shoved them in his face. He knew well that he was in danger. But he couldn't believe that his father-in-law was having him followed.

Mr. Salvador asked Cane one question: "How long do you think I'd let you drag my family through the mud?" Cane had a shivering expression on his face because he knew what was going to happen to him. He just wasn't ready to say goodbye to Glow and their Baby Girl; images of them flashed before his eyes. The only thing he could do was mentally say goodbye.

Mr. Salvador directed one of his bodyguards to restrain Cane. Then they dragged him down into the cellar and tortured him for five days. Mr. Salvador wanted Cane to feel the agony he caused his daughter with his two young sons' watches. Cane's pain, however, would be physical rather than emotional.

Cane was aware that Mr. Salvador had a couple of Pitbulls roaming the grounds, but he never imagined that he would become the dog's meal of the day.

Mr. Salvador hired a hooker to get Cane on hard for the Pitbulls. The bodyguards had already stripped him naked. Cane was up and running after the hooker finished her work. The bodyguards gave the hooker hamburger meat to wrap around Cane's penis.

When the hooker did as she was told, one bodyguard dismissed her, forgetting what she had seen. One bodyguard wrapped a chain around Cane's neck; what happened next was incredible. Another bodyguard, they called Killer, was insane. Killer extracted Cane's eyeballs, rubbed red pepper on them, and fed them to the Pitbull's.

Cane was swinging from a beam in the middle of the floor as the bodyguards pounded on him until he passed out. Because Cane had lost so much blood, they assumed he was dead. However, Killer and his crew were sitting around when they heard a noise coming from Cane; the Pit-bull's remained. Also, they wrapped the hamburger meat around Cane's penis again for the dogs to eat, and the Pitbull's chewed on Cane's penis until he passed out again.

Cane regained consciousness, the chain around his neck so tight that he was choking on his own blood. Mr. Salvador ordered that the body be removed and the head be boxed up. They send it to his new wife as a warning not to mess with the Salvador's.

Silk didn't want Glow to learn about Cane's secret life before he cleared his name from the suspect list. Unfortunately, it wasn't long before Glow relapsed into some of her bad habits. Silk knew he needed to gain her trust to gain access to some of the fortune Cane had left behind.

Silk had no idea Cane's Baby Girl was being groomed to take over her father's empire; she was growing up fast. Cane had been dead for a year, and Baby Girl had grown up like a tweed.

Silk came over to talk to Glow one day. Glow was devastated by Cane's death, and she was never the same after that. She began drinking excessively, allowing her appearance to deteriorate and her weight to drop; she had to pull herself together for Baby Girl.

Glow stepped out of the living room, where she and Silk were conversing, answering her phone. Silk spiced her drink while she was out of the room; it was his way of alerting Glow to her misfortune. Silk had no idea Glow had cameras installed in every room of her house. As a result, she kept a close eye on Silk's every move.

Silk was sitting in the living room with a half-smile on his face when Glow entered. She wanted to turn his upside-down smile off, but she knew it wasn't the right time or place. She had big plans for Silk.

One night only. Glow was sound asleep in her bedroom when a vision of Cane appeared in the doorway. He looked just as good to her as he did the day he left for his two-week trip. However, something about the image threw her off; he appeared worried, and his skin was pale.

Cane led Glow to the center of the room, where he kept the floor safe and put his fingers up to give her the combination to the safe. She couldn't believe what she was seeing, because he had never previously told her about the safe.

Glow was devastated when she unlocked the safe. She saw documents from the Hawaiian crime family that she could bury them with. It was incriminating evidence about Cane's business. She also discovered from those documents that Silk is Cane's son from another crackhead he met before joining the mafia family.

Silk had no idea Cane was his father. Because Cane had Silk's mother murdered for threatening to tell the mafia family and his wife Rakia about their bastard son. Cane couldn't have that, so the only way he could ensure it didn't happen was to make Silk's mother take a permanent dirt nap.

Glow also discovered documents that would ensure Baby Girl's safety for the rest of her life. She had photos of everyone in the mafia family, so she knew Cane had left all of that information to protect himself and their daughter. There was also a map to a safe house, in case she ever needed to visit it.

Cane explained in a letter about his poor choices and misfortunes in life. His father was a pimp, and his mother was a drug addict who sold him to the highest bidder. He would not have known her if it hadn't been for this old man in the Hawaiian village where he was born. He was saved by the old man.

Cane also cautioned Glow not to trust Silk and to keep their daughter safe at all costs. Glow spent the night going over all the data she had. She then decided it was time to make a plan for her daughter in case something went wrong. But, first, she wanted to make sure that Baby Girl had the information Cane had given her.

After two days, Glow had not heard from Silk, which made her nervous. So she made a few phone calls to find out where Silk was. If only she had known Silk had simply stayed and camped outside Glow's house, a few houses down, in an unmarked car. Keeping his gaze fixed on his fortune.

Silk's mind was wandering with ideas of how he could devise a master plan that was not so obvious to Glow. Silk had a feeling Glow was spying on him. Suddenly, he realized he could get on Glow's good side by arranging a drug bust for her. Silk wasn't attempting to remove Glow entirely from the picture. He only wanted what was rightfully his.

He believed that because he had set up Cane and now that Cane was dead; he deserved Cane's empire. Silk remained hidden for a while. He didn't want to appear desperate, so he invited Glow to come to him. Silk had no idea Glow was planning on doing just that. She had her own plans for Silk's demise.

Silk was mainly in hiding because he was on the phone with one of Mr. Salvador's bodyguards one day. Tony, one of Cane's foot soldiers, overheard their conversation about Cane's demise. Silk had no idea what the foot soldier had heard, but he knew it was enough to get him killed if Glow found out.

Silk was unaware of Tony's situation. Tony was also Cane's son. Neither of them was aware of any connection between them. Tony knew well that what he was keeping from Glow would either break her down or tear her apart. He had never put his trust in Silk. The first day Cane brought him on set, he sensed something was wrong with him. So, before approaching Glow with any information, he had to be sure of his facts.

Tony waited another day before calling Glow and asking to meet with her about some serious business. She hadn't heard from Tony in a while, so Glow agreed to meet with him to find out what he had to say.

Glow asked Tony to meet her at Club Sexy downtown. He asked Glow what time it was, and she told Tony to arrive at 7:30 a.m., to which he agreed. Glow was relieved to see Tony because he was devoted to her and Cane. She knew she could put her life in Tony's hands.

Glow ordered drinks of their choice, and the conversation began with Tony complimenting Glow on her beauty. Then he inquired about her daughter's well-being. Glow stated her daughter was in good health.

"I know you didn't call this meeting to question me about my daughter, so what's the actual story, Tony?"

"Well foremost, I'd like to inquire whether you've heard from Silk recently."

"No. Have you done so?"

"No. But I know Silk set up Cane's murder by the mafia family."

Glow initially sat there staring at Tony. He had to have known something; she reasoned. Tony wouldn't know about the mafia if she didn't tell him unless Tony and Cane were much closer than she imagined.

"Glow, are you okay because all the color just disappeared from your face?"

"I'm fine, Tony. I'm fine. Stop blathering and get on with the story."

"I was supposed to be on the set that day Cane left for his two-week vacation, but I left late because I had the bubble guts when I woke up that morning."

"I thought I was alone in the house until I heard voices coming from Cane's office in the back. Of course, everyone knows not to enter Cane's office or touch his private phone line. So I stood near the door to hear who was in Cane's office. When I heard Silk's voice, I knew something was up. So I waited quietly to hear what Silk had to say. The next thing I heard Silk say blew me away. Silk was essentially carrying out a hit on the man he was supposed to protect with his life."

Tony knew Silk wasn't a jerk at first, but who was going to believe him? Occasionally, Tony attempted to confront Cane about Silk's evil ways. Still, he wouldn't listen, because Silk and Tony were constantly competing for Cane's attention. If it wasn't about driving Cane around to find the best dope spot for the day.

Glow was intent on the conversation she was having with Tony. So she inquired about his knowledge of the Italian mafia. Tony's knowledge was devastating to Glow because he appears to be faithful to her. It was the same information she had read in the information Cane had left for her in the safe.

What perplexed Glow the most was how this man could claim to love her while living a double life. Glow felt stupid because she couldn't have known him despite living with him. So Tony and Glow banded together that day to handle their business with Silk.

After three days, Silk carried out his plan. He stole two dope keys from the dope house along with three AK-47s and planted them in Glow's place. Silk had to get into Glow's house undetected because they had armed her house like Fort Knox's.

Silk devised the plan to cut the wires to the cameras and alarm systems. He knew he wouldn't have any trouble getting in after that. So he learned to choose the day when Baby Girl would be at school and Glow would be at Club Sexy.

Two days later, Glow got out of bed, made breakfast, drove Baby Girl to school, and went to Club Sexy. Glow went to Club Sexy twice a week to make sure everything was in order. However, she felt a cold chill run down her spine after leaving Club Sexy that day, causing her to break out in a sweat. She had a feeling something wasn't quite right. She had the impression that she was being followed.

Glow recalled a ride she and Cane had taken. Cane thought he was being followed, so he pulled into a gas station. She did the same thing to see if her feminine intuition kicked in. When Glow arrived at the station, the car continued on its way. That was fine with her, but her feminine instincts were still tingling.

Glow called Tony to find out what was wrong with him, and she told him she was being followed by someone driving a dark blue charger with no plates. Tony had no idea who it was, but he warned Glow to be cautious, just in case Silk was still in the city. Glow told Tony she would and asked him to do the same, and they hung up saying nothing else.

Glow knew she and Tony were on the same page; something wasn't right. So after she hung up with Tony, she went shopping at the mall because Baby Girl needed new clothes. Unfortunately, while Glow was at the mall, Silk was buzzing around Glow's house, trying to persuade himself to turn off the cameras and alarm systems.

Glow was at the checkout counter, paying for her daughter's clothes, when she felt compelled to return home. So she hopped in her charger, hit the highway, and drove home. Silk was about to enter her house through the back door when he heard the garage door slide open just in time.

Silk slid down to the ground and crept into the bushes. He moved to the side of the house where Glow couldn't see him. Silk returned to the street where he had parked his unmarked car. Silk thought to himself as he looked in his rearview mirror. "Damn! I almost got caught. What if she checked the wires or something?"

Silk went back to the drawing board, knowing he needed to devise a solid plan and an escape route. However, he was unaware that Glow had a lady who lived across the street watching the house for her.

Glow summoned a repairman to reconnect the cameras and alarm systems. Then she contacted Tony to collaborate on a plan to remove Silk from the map.

Tony stopped by Glow's house that night to talk about the plan. His plan was to drag Silk to a drug meeting and use it as leverage to get what he wanted. Tony knew it was risky. Silk had been hunting for Tony since he had peered at him and overheard his conversation with the mafia family.

Tony explained to Glow how the plan would work. It delighted her to be a part of Silk's dirt nap. Tony informed Glow it would be an actual drug transaction, so they would need at least $50,000 to carry out the plan.

Glow assured Tony that this would be possible. What Glow didn't know for sure was how it would all play out. Glow took one of the AK-47s and two extra clips just to be safe; she preferred to be safe than sorry.

When Tony called Silk to schedule the meeting, Silk agreed to meet him at Cane's remote warehouse. Tony understood what Silk was saying because there was nothing but dirt roads and trees out there. When Cane was still alive, they had killed and chopped up many people out there.

Silk summoned Short Stack, another foot soldier he can rely on. Short Stack works for Cane and dislikes Tony because he thinks Tony is an ass-kissing Uncle Tom.

So when Silk called to let Short Stack know what was going on, he was ready: He told Silk he had been waiting for the opportunity to put two in Tony's head.

While Tony and Glow were gathering their firepower on the Westside of town, Silk and Short Stack were doing the same. Silk ran down to Short

Stack to tell him about the situation with Glow, but he didn't tell him about the money because he didn't have to. However, everyone in Cane's drug business was aware of what was going on.

Short Stack had his own plan as well. He summoned his twin brother, Snake, to accompany him and monitor his back. As Short Stack was explaining the situation to his brother, the phone rang, and it was Silk telling him it was time to bounce.

Short Stack told his brother that he would be at his house in ten minutes to get his guns and go outside. Unfortunately, Glow and Tony were already at the warehouse waiting for Silk's arrival, unaware that Silk had backup. When Silk arrived at the warehouse, he noticed Tony's car parked, so he told Short Stack to give him twenty minutes before approaching him.

Tony emerged from behind the lumber they had against the wall as Silk entered the warehouse.

"Where's the money, Tony?" Silk inquired.

"I have the money. Where are the drugs?" Tony replied.

Silk kept reaching for Tony's side, showing that something was about to happen. Tony was about to say something else when Short Stack and Snake charged in, blazing, hitting Silk and Tony ripping Silk apart. Tony fell behind the lumber, and Glow fired the AK-47 at Short Stack and Snake so fast they didn't even notice.

Before she left, Glow assisted Tony in exiting the warehouse. Foremost, she wanted to ensure that Silk and his sidekicks were dead. Then, once Glow had Tony in the car, she returned to the warehouse to ensure that neither she nor Tony had left any trace of their presence. Unfortunately, Tony had passed out by the time Glow returned to the car. She was at a loss for what to do. Then she remembered the doctor Cane had seen about a gunshot wound, so she summoned him to her house to care for Tony.

Tony had been shot three times, once in the chest and twice in the abdomen. He was losing blood quickly, which worried Glow. Tony was going to die. He was still out cold by the time the doctor arrived. Despite this, the doctor performed emergency surgery on Tony in Glow's garage.

He extracted the bullets and gave Glow pain relievers for Tony. The doctor was ten thousand dollars richer when he left.

Glow felt relieved that she no longer had to monitor Silk because Silk was already taking a dirt nap, or so she thought. She waited for the news that night because she wanted to know what happened at the warehouse. However, it did not air until the second day. Then, finally, it was broadcast on television. Glow was preparing dinner for herself and her daughter in the kitchen. When the news broke, the warehouse shooting of two guys known as Short Stack and Snake, their street names. Because it ripped their bodies to shreds, no one could identify them. She became concerned because the news only mentioned two men, not three. Glow knew she had to get Baby Girl to a safe place.

Glow took her daughter to the safe house that Cane had written about. She was taken aback when she arrived. The location was lovely, and the fridge was stocked with food. Glow knew they couldn't stay hidden for long because her daughter needed to go to school.

Glow doesn't have any family in Chicago, so she needed to develop a plan. But first, she needed to get her daughter out of town and into a safe place.

Glow was sitting there thinking when something flashed through her mind. She reflected on her aunt Marie, who was still in Ohio. She was friendly with Glow until the state intervened and took her away after her mother was murdered. Glow simply didn't know how she was going to approach her aunt. She hadn't seen her aunt Marie in years. She didn't even know if she's still alive, but she had to try.

Glow went to the white pages to see if she could find her aunt's address and phone number, and lo-and-behold, she did. So she dialed her Aunt Marie's number and talked for hours. Then she invited Glow to pay her a visit soon. She did not know Glow would be there to see her sooner than she expected.

Glow was on a plane two days later, taking her Baby Girl to see her aunt Marie. When she arrived, she rented a car and drove to Aunt Marie's house, where she was delighted to see Aunt Marie, who was doing very well for herself. Aunt Marie then heard a knock on her door. When she opened the door and saw Glow standing there with this lovely little girl, it reminded her of when the state department brought Glow to her house. Aunt Marie burst into tears of joy. However, the expression on Glow's face told her that something wasn't right.

After Aunt Marie had fed them lunch, she asked Angel if she wanted to watch television while she spoke with her mother. Aunt Marie looked at Glow and asked what was wrong with her. Because she knew something had to be bad for her to show up at her door after ten years. Glow told Aunt Marie about her life, from being a crackhead to marrying a Hawaiian kingpin.

Glow even told her aunt about Cane's head being delivered in a box to her house. Glow gave Aunt Marie instructions, just in case she didn't return to get her daughter. She also left her a bank account to care for her Baby Girl. Aunt Marie assured Glow she would take care of her daughter with her life and that she would not have to worry about her as long as she lived.

Glow stayed the night, awoke the next day, and returned to Chicago. Glow returned the car she rented and boarded the next flight to Chicago. She had a strange feeling in her stomach when she arrived in Chicago. She felt as if all eyes were on her. Glow was all too familiar with that sensation. She knew she had to find Silk's whereabouts quickly because she didn't want to keep looking behind her back. What Glow didn't realize was that Tony was on the case while she was in hiding: he had spied Silk in an unmarked dark blue sedan parked down the street from Glow's house.

Tony had already set Silk up for a trap. He wanted Silk to suffer gradually for what he had done to Cane. Tony was waiting for it to get dark, to sneak up behind Silk and rock him to sleep. That way, he'd be able to take him somewhere private. Silk sat in his car down the block, waiting for Glow to return. Then, suddenly, he felt a sharp pain in his neck. Tony had snuck into Silk's car when he got out to pee.

Tony couldn't believe his good fortune: he tied Silk up, took him to an empty house, and waited for Glow to call. After four hours. Glow was on her way to the abandoned house. Silk was wide awake from the heroin Tony had shot in his neck when Glow arrived at the house. Silk looked up and saw Glow, and he began pleading for his life because he knew Glow was up to no good.

Glow asked Silk what Cane had done to him to cause him to set him up the way he did. Glow was taken aback by what Silk said next.

"That bastard killed my mother," he told Glow. Cane didn't want me to know I was his son. I discovered I was his son after snooping around in his office one day. His safe held my birth certificate. "The dumbass fucker should have concealed it better."

"Go ahead, bitch. Kill me. I ain't got shit. I'm better off dead, anyway. But before you do, I want you to know Mr. Salvador knows about you and your daughter, and he's going to kill both of y'all."

Glow got so upset with that statement. She slapped the shit out of Silk because he did not know she knew about Mr. Salvador and his whole mafia family.

"That's enough talking," Tony said. It's time for Silk to meet his maker."

Tony poured a large can of battery acid all over Silk's body. Slowly, he wished to hear him scream in agony. Tony began by smearing the acid on Silk's face. Like hot grease at a fish fry, it melted his skin off.

There was nothing to clean up after Tony finished with Silk; Silk was history. Glow and Tony walked away from the abandoned house, never speaking of Silk again. However, following the death of Silk, they became close friends.

Three

~

The Death of Gloria Carter a.k.a. Glow

Glow wanted to head over to her Aunt Marie's house to pick up her daughter. Her plan was to do it after she'd taken care of some personal matters. However, she was not confident that she was completely safe. She didn't think it was safe for her to return home either.

Glow felt lonely one night as she sat looking at pictures of herself and Cane. She realized she needed company to stay on track. Unfortunately, she had no female acquaintances, and Tony was the only person she knew who might assist her. She didn't want to bother him, but she desperately needed someone to talk to.

Glow was about to call Tony when she heard a knock on the door. She peered through the keyhole to see Tony standing there with a bottle of Moet & Chandon.

"You must have been reading my mind. I was about to call you to find out what you were doing." She said.

What Glow didn't realize was that Tony had his own agenda. He, too, wished to get a little closer to Glow. He wondered why a kingpin like

Cane married a crackhead like Glow. Was it because she was smart or good in bed?

Tony reasoned that if he could get her drunk enough, she might share. Tony wished to be Glow's lover, but he knew he was probably too young. But he kept his thoughts to himself. Of course, nothing beats success, but what harm can a try cause?

Glow and Tony sat there all night getting toasted. Then, finally, when he raised his head, Glow said she needed to use the restroom, and she'd be right back.

Glow returned to the room dressed in a long silk gown with nothing underneath. Tony gave her a wide-eyed stare, recognizing the tune. Tony was getting ready to go balls deep, and Glow did things to him he had never imagined.

The following day, Tony woke up to breakfast in bed. He was beaming as if he had won the lottery.

Glow asked Tony. "What do you want to do today?"

"Glow, whatever you want to do. I'll deal with it." He replied.

Glow and Tony had been going strong for about two months when Glow noticed she was missing her period again. Glow knew she couldn't have another child with him. She was lonely and had no idea this short romance would last so long.

Glow went to the pharmacy to get a pregnancy test while Tony was gone. She wanted to make sure she wasn't pregnant because if she was; she was going to the abortion clinic right away. Glow didn't want to give Tony the satisfaction of believing he'd be a father, especially since she was the mother. She had no idea whether Tony had kids, and she didn't care because he was just her playmate.

Tony had gone to the store to get her some roses. When Tony made it back to Glow's house, Glow was still in the bathroom. She was waiting for the results of her pregnancy test. Tony yelled her name as he walked in to make sure she was still there.

Glow was so preoccupied that she didn't hear Tony call her name. Instead, she was in her room on the phone making an appointment to abort the baby she was carrying. Then she remembered the pregnancy test kit still on the bathroom sink. Glow was about to return to the bathroom to get it when Tony turned to her. She was in shock because Tony was holding the test stick that read positive.

"Are we having a baby?" Tony asked.

"No, sweetheart, we're not." She replied.

Tony looked at Glow as if she was sprouting two heads.

"Yes, we are, because I don't have any children," Tony said.

Glow informed Tony that she was not paying attention because the situation was not her concern. She also told him he could find another woman to be the mother of his children if he so desired. She had her own child, and that was all she needed.

Tony was devastated. For the first time in his life, he had a purpose, and he would not allow her to deprive him of it. He was so enraged that he abandoned Glow's home and did not contact her for two weeks. Finally, Tony attempted to persuade Glow to have his child, unaware that Glow had already aborted the child. When Glow told Tony the baby had been taken, he punched the wall, breaking two of his knuckles; he was furious. Glow startled when she heard the noise. She hadn't expected Tony to take it so personally, but he did.

Tony was so angry at Glow that he began having nightmares about a crying baby. It drove him crazy. He wanted to retaliate against Glow and even considered killing her daughter. But he fought the thought because Baby Girl had nothing to do with her mother's wrongdoings. However, he would make Glow pay for aborting his child. He only needed to devise a strategy to re-establish his relationship with her since Glow had stopped talking to him.

Glow tried to carry on with her life. She even went to her Aunt Marie and picked up her daughter. They were happy for a while until one night when she was on her way home from Club Sexy. Glow felt as if she was being followed. She looked in her rearview mirror and noticed a black expedition with bright lights close behind her. She sped up to make sure if she was really being followed this time. But, to her surprise, she was being followed by mafia hitmen. Mr. Salvador discovered that Silk, his inside source for her and her daughter, had been murdered by Glow.

Glow was going so fast that she missed her turn. So she took a dark alley, pulled into someone's carport, and waited for the car to pass. After the car passed and it was safe for her to leave, Glow went home to call Tony. She hadn't spoken to Tony in over three months because of the baby. Glow reasoned Tony could at the very least protect her. He was the only person on whom she could rely. However, Tony had gone dark and was now working for Mr. Salvador, which Glow was unaware of.

If only she'd known that when she called Tony, he was in the car with Mr. Salvador's hitman, Killer. Killer and Mr. Salvador's other bodyguards murdered Cane. Glow was in a lot of trouble. She had no idea that the person she trusted the most would bring her down.

Tony responded to Glow's call as if he was relieved to hear her voice. He adored Glow, but she cut him when she took away his child. That was something he couldn't forgive her for. She invited Tony to come over.

"There's something I need to talk to you about. Please come. It's an emergency." Glow told Tony.

Tony nodded and continued on his way.

Tony inquired about Glow's daughter when he arrived at her home. She informed him she was sleeping in her bedroom. Glow told Tony of what had just happened. Tony wasn't surprised because he knew he was at the center of it all. His mouth was dry, and he needed to clear his throat. So Tony requested Glow get him something to drink, which she did. Glow went to get a bottle of water. When she returned to the living room, she came to a halt. Tony was standing next to Killer, holding a knife to her daughter's throat.

"Please, she has nothing to do with this," Glow begged Tony as she dropped the bottle of water.

"You deal with her, and I'll be in the other room with her daughter," Killer told Tony.

Tony expected killing Glow would be simple. But he was the one who charged forward with a hammer and smacked Glow in the face. She landed on a glass coffee table, which split her back when she fell to the floor. Tony bent over to check her pulse. Glow was still breathing, so he wrapped a guitar string around her neck until she stopped.

Before Killer left Glow's house with Baby Girl wrapped in a blanket, he knew he could not leave Tony alive as a witness to Glow's death or Angel's kidnapping. So Killer took Baby Girl to the car. She was still sleeping, so she left her in the backseat, with the driver sitting up under the steering wheel, ready to hit the gas at any moment.

Killer knew well that Tony was about to go out in a blaze of glory. He injected heroin into the needle, and Tony closed his eyes to see a vision of his mother, whom he had never met. Tony was only two weeks old when he was dropped off at the hospital's door. Tony was completely alone; he didn't have any family. So it makes no difference what happens to him. He thought he had something to live for when he found out Glow was pregnant. But that went down like shit in the toilet.

Baby Girl ended up being raised by Mr. Salvador after Glow's death. She'll be groomed to be a hustling diva, to run the Chicago area as her father did.

Four

~

Angel a.k.a. Baby Girl

As the mafia princess, Baby Girl grew up in a mansion fit for a king. She grew up with her brothers, Dante and David, Cane's sons from Rakia. Angel's name had been changed to protect her innocence from the cops who were searching for her after discovering her mother brutally murdered.

The police had issued an all-points bulletin in order to locate Angel Carter. They had no idea Angel would never use that alias again. She will, however, appear on a wanted poster in Chicago years later.

Angel attended the most prestigious schools and graduated with distinction. She had the best cars and was lavishly spoiled by her new family. Her brothers were devoted to her. For them, she was the most beautiful girl they'd ever seen, aside from their mother.

Everyone knew Mr. Salvador wasn't someone to play with. Angel was his royal granddaughter and was never teased at school. She attended college with two high school friends. They were inseparable and did everything together.

Gabriel was Italian and black, and she was also born into the mafia. Mr. Giovanni, her father, was the head of the Detroit area. She, too, had been spoiled rotten. Gabriel had the most beautiful smooth skin Angel had ever seen. She is 5'7", had long curly hair, green eyes, and weighed 125 pounds.

Her other girlfriend's name was Abby, and she, too, was of mixed race. Her father was white, and her mother was African-American. Abby was born into wealth because her father was an ob-gyn doctor and her mother was a criminal attorney. She towered over Angel and Gabriel. She stood six feet tall, had long brown hair, green eyes, and fair skin. Abby looks like Jennifer Lopez's twin sister.

Angel was overjoyed to be the Salvador family's number one girl. When she graduated from college, she became accustomed to their way of life. Mr. Salvador then called a meeting with his granddaughter Angel and grandsons Dante and David one day. They had reached the right age to run the family business, and it was time for them to spread their wings.

Mr. Salvador manages six buildings in Chicago, so each of them had two to manage. So when Angel, Dante, and David were summoned for dinner, they were all assigned tasks. Angel hated leaving her friends behind, but she had to. Angel thus abandoned her friends, only to be reunited with them six months later.

By the time Gabriel and Abby arrived in Chicago, the threesome had the city figured out. David and Dante, like soldiers, became involved in the drug trade. To the twins, the dope gang was a piece of cake. The other dope boys on the set were terrified by how much they resembled Cane. It was like looking into a mirror. They were more powerful than their father's drug gang because David was an accountant and Dante was deeply involved in politics.

They were all raised to be moneymakers. To avoid being ruled by money, they were involved in drug distribution, firearms sales, prostitution, selling black market babies, and other illegal activities. They did whatever brings in money. They even had a warehouse full of furs where fur coats being sold like lottery tickets.

Angel needed to go to the airport to meet up with her friends. They were stuck in their tracks as she approached the drop-off curve. In a baby blue Rolls-Royce, she rolled up on them.

"Damn! Abby exclaimed to Angel. They haven't started making those yet, girl."

"Know somebody who knows somebody, girl," Angel said.

What they didn't realize was that when Angel landed in Chicago, she hit the ground running. She knew exactly how to run their organization. Her twin brothers and she met once a week to compare notes and ensure they were on the same page. They only needed to communicate with Mr. Salvador once a month. Then they could only call once every six months if they had problems.

Dante's and David's businesses ran like clockwork. They had to start by hiring madams for their whorehouses. Then they'd go to top-tier private parties where they knew there were top-tier call girls they could hire to be madams. The women there were stunning and knew exactly how they wanted them to be. If not, they had already made plans to train them to be the best madams the Chicago area had ever seen.

When they arrived in Chicago, Dante put an attorney on retainer in case they needed one. Dante had no idea they'd become best friends, or that the attorney he had on retainer was as shady as they come. He was also involved in a variety of activities.

Mike Trivet was a black lawyer who struggled through law school. He even killed a couple of people to get there. Growing up poor in the hood earned him brownie points. He did his dirty work on the sly so no one would notice. Mike was not married, but he had two sons from previous relationships with two different women. He wasn't seeing anyone at the moment, just playing around on the field until he ran into Miss Right.

Mike was a tall, handsome, well-dressed man with a low-cut face and stunning hazel-green eyes. He was born and raised on Austin's Lower West Side. When he was twelve, his mother died of a drug overdose. His grandmother raised him until she died of a stroke when he was eighteen, leaving him to fend for himself on the streets. He never met his father because his grandmother disliked his father and would never allow him to be near Mike.

Dante and Mike met for the first time at a lawyer's convention. Dante was there to make his selection, looking for someone with a bit of swagger. In the meeting, he noticed Mike, and something about him stood out like a sore thumb. This guy looks familiar, Dante kept telling himself. He appears to be related to me.

Dante knew Mike had to be on his payroll after their first encounter. But he also knew that David and Angel needed to meet with him because they all needed to agree with Mike as their attorney. So he just hoped they saw what he saw because he could be related for real.

Dante planned a dinner date for the three of them and Mike to know each other better. They were also taken aback when they arrived at the restaurant because he appeared so familiar to them. They couldn't find him, so they left him alone for the time being. Angel's two friends accompanied her to dinner, and they were captivated by Mike's sexiness. They weren't sure who would yell at Mike, but they knew one of them would give Mr. Trivet a run for his money.

That evening's meeting went well. They all agreed to keep Mike on retainer after considering what their grandfather had told them. Mr. Salvador told them to act as if they had no kin or ties to the mafia family once they arrived in Chicago. As a result, they had to handle their own affairs. Unless it was a life-or-death situation, which was the only time they could contact him. Aside from that, they only did mafia business with Killer.

Angel's twenty-third birthday was approaching. Dante and David were planning a big birthday bash for her at Club Sexy, the hottest club in the tristate area. They wanted to go all out for their little sister, so they hired her favorite singer, Keyshia Cole, to perform as a surprise at her party. David tells Angel's friends, Abby and Gabriel, about the surprise so they can keep her occupied for the day. David told them to take her shopping and to the spa, which would make her happy. Angel loved to shop, so she wouldn't say no to that.

"Stop playing, twin, Abby said. Isn't it true that every female enjoys going shopping?"

David reached into his wallet, pulled out a black MasterCard with a $200,000 limit, and said, "Go crazy. Make my sister look like a princess."

While David was busy keeping Angel occupied, Dante was setting up Club Sexy for the party that night. He had taken care of the music first, and now he was working on the decorations. He didn't know any decorators, so he called Mike to see if he could recommend any. Yes, Mike said, and he'd have someone at Club Sexy in twenty minutes. So that was the end of that part, and Dante could breathe again. It was time to start the party after Abby, Gabriel, and Angel had finished shopping and going to the spa.

Gabriel needed to devise a strategy to get Angel out of the house for the party. Especially since Angel stated she was tired and wanted to nap. Gabriel only had two hours to get Angel to her surprise birthday party.

Even though Angel didn't think they had plans to go out that evening, they knew they'd be the shit at Club Sexy. Abby and Gabriel had already showered when Angel awoke from a thirty-minute nap. They were straightening each other's hair. They didn't have enough time to get to the beauty salon, but that was fine because their hair was naturally straight.

They eventually persuaded Angel to accompany them to the club. All three girls wore three-thousand-dollar gowns with matching two-thousand-dollar shoes and handbags. They all looked stunning as they entered the club, and all eyes were on them. When Angel walked into the club, the people there sang in surprise. She burst into tears. She assumed her brothers had forgotten about her birthday because they did not even acknowledge it that day.

When the ample bright light lit up on stage, the party kicked into high gear. Angel had no idea what was going on until they announced Keyshia Cole would be on stage. Angel really broke down. Dante thought he needed to take her to the emergency room, but she was fine. She thanked her brothers repeatedly for their unconditional love for her.

Five

～

Terror and Destruction

It's time to get back to work now that the party is over. Angel needed to gather her men because two shipments of cocaine were due to arrive the next day.

Angel demanded the best, so she assembled a fearsome squad of soldiers. She'll have undercover cops train them, take them to shooting ranges, and teach them how to use high-powered weapons with silencers, scopes, and night vision goggles. Angel wanted her soldiers to be unstoppable, so she mandated that they all wear bulletproof vests. Angel also had two judges, cops, detectives, and the prosecutor on her payroll, so she had Chicago under her control.

Angel envisioned building an empire from the ground up. Being bred by the head of a mafia family, she wanted her family's patriarch to be proud of her and her brothers, so she summoned Killer to gather fifty more terrifying men from all over the world.

A wanted black man's photo appeared on TV immediately after she hung up with Killer. Cortez Smith, alias Killer Perez, struck a chord with her. He had a mug that would frighten even the dead, and she needed this guy as her soldier, so she had to track him down.

She needed to hire a private investigator to find Killer Perez. Mike eventually introduced her to Deacon Hayes, and he demanded $2,000 an hour, which she accepted. Angel smiled as she left Deacon Hayes' office, having heard good things about him from Mike. Mike told her he could poke a hole in cotton.

Angel had only two weeks to gather her army. Killer contacted and informed her that her team would be on their way in a week. So she ordered her cops on standby until they were ready. Angel made one more call to her brothers. Her players were ready, and it's time to put the city in terror and destruction.

Dante and David were also assembling their troops on the other side of town. They agreed to have undercover retired police officers serve as their soldiers, and they carefully planned their strategy.

Dante inquired of Mike about their decision, and he encouraged him to go for it. *What could they possibly lose? They were trained and knew the neighborhood well.* Plus, Mike knew who they needed precisely.

Dante and David scheduled a meeting with Mike and the retired cops. They wanted to know if they were interested in becoming dark side soldiers.

When Dante and David arrived at the meeting, the retired officers were shocked by how much the twins resembled the missing Hawaiian kingpin, Cane Carter. But they didn't mind because they needed the money.

Dante and David needed to protect the drug houses and whorehouses, so they agreed to settle on a weekly salary of $2,000. However, they also needed one in command, so they tested them to find the deserving.

The twins wanted the retired cops to kill their eldest child to prove their worth. They didn't care about them or their families. The twins were serious about their business, and nothing or no one would stand their way. To run an empire, they would kill crawling babies if necessary.

The retired cops told them they were sick and should go to hell except for one officer named Hammer. Hammer stayed on board because the man was insane and a sick individual for real. He had three crazy sons who were always in trouble. Montello, his eldest, was a vengeful son of a bitch who despised Hammer with a vengeance. So Hammer could send his firstborn child to hell without issue.

To ensure Hammer would do what they asked, Dante and David sent Mike along with him. He was to return with the head of his firstborn child, pictures, and a birth certificate naming Hammer as his biological father.

Hammer returned home that evening with his son's head in a plastic bag inside a box. He accomplished his goal with no regrets. They knew they had a crazy-ass lunatic on their team, but the twins also knew they had to monitor him.

Meanwhile, Angel had her soldiers, and they were in training on the other side of town. Angel and her girls were on their way to the military store to buy over a hundred bulletproof vests. When they walked in, she knew her plan to get the artillery she wanted would go off with a bang.

Angel had reserved one of her buildings for pregnant runaway teens. She was preparing to sell babies on the black market. She had already let four pregnant girls move into her building because they had nowhere else to go.

Amy, Dina, Alexandra, and Cynthia were close friends. They were all pregnant and living on the street when they met Angel. They thought Angel pities them, but Angel had other plans. Angel took them home that day and let them stay in one of her buildings.

Angel took great care of the girls' needs, including feeding, clothing, and doctor visits. The girls were relieved they weren't pillars anymore. They thought Angel was their pal, but they did not know Angel planned to sell their babies on the black market.

Amy, Alexandra, and Cynthia still had four months to go, but Dina was due any day now. Angel had already set up her website and printed out their pictures and health reports for the expecting parents to see. She knew what each girl was having, and the expectant parents were excited, awaiting their child. Angel wanted $100,000 for each kid. She was recouping her room, board, and medical expenses.

Dina gave birth on a hot July night, and her screams woke up the other girls. Angel advised them to go back to bed because she could handle it.

Angel took Dina to the basement, set up as a maternity ward. It had every tool a doctor needed to deliver babies. Angel had a doctor on staff, but he wasn't an ob-gyn, so he couldn't deliver babies.

Angel only cared about the babies. She didn't care about the mothers; she just wanted healthy babies. When Angel let the girls move in, she knew they wouldn't make it out alive. Dina's baby was having trouble descending and breached, so the doctor had to shoot. The doctor drew Angel out into the hallway and told her he was helpless.

"What the hell do you mean? You're a damn doctor, aren't you?" Angel exclaimed.

"Yes, I specialize in gunshot wounds, not in delivering babies." The doctor explained.

Angel erupted. She cut the doctor's throat without thinking, leaving Dina bleeding to death on the delivery table. Angel heard her scream and used the same scalpel to cut open Dina's stomach and remove the baby.

Angel wrapped the baby in a blanket and placed him in the crib while she checked on Dina. She saw Dina's eyes and knew she was half-dead, so she took the drill from the table and chopped off her head. Angel began dismembering Dina. Angel was helpless when the baby started crying, so she picked him up and gave him a chilled milk bottle to stop him from crying.

Angel called her friends and told them one baby was born, but the mother died. She didn't want Abby or Gabriel to know she was a born killer just yet. However, Dina's roommates were curious about her and her baby's whereabouts, so they asked Angel. Angel told them Dina took her baby and moved back in with her mother to avoid raising him alone.

Three days after Dina's disappearance, Cynthia asked the other two girls. "Do you think Dina went back to her mother's house? Remember Dina saying her mother died in a house fire when we were homeless?"

They all paused and said, "true, something is wrong, and we need to know what happened to Dina."

The months flew by, and the girls' bellies exploded. They both went into labor four days apart, except for Amy. She wasn't going anywhere. Her contractions were 15 minutes apart later that night.

Amy got up and snuck out. She wanted her baby and didn't want to be like Dina, so she ran until she passed out in front of a grocery store.

Amy awoke in the hospital. She had an eight-pound-ten-ounce baby boy named Conner. Amy told no one what happened in the hell house, and she never saw Alexandra or Cynthia again.

Amy stayed in town, got a job at a thrift shop, and quickly became the manager. Excuse me, could you please help me? A man said behind her as she was installing recent signs. Amy almost fainted when she turned around to see him because he was so handsome.

"Hi, my name is Amy." she said.

"Hi, my name is David." He replied.

David ordered 100 army fictive uniforms for his soldiers. David called Amy the following day and invited her for a dinner date, which she agreed. So he told Amy he'd pick her up at 8:30 for dinner, and Amy said she'd be ready and gave him her address.

David and Amy had a wonderful dinner. They talked nicely and kept looking into each other's eyes. They both needed each other. David was exhausted from running his empire, and Amy was worried about running from Angel on the streets. She, too, needed a breath of fresh air. So David and Amy had a hot and heavy affair for a couple of months.

Angel gave an introduction dance for their soldiers one night when she noticed a woman entering the room with David. Her heart almost jumped out of her chest. Her eyes had to be playing tricks on her.

That can't be Amy on her brother's arm! *"I have to get her to meet me in the bathroom because I bet she hasn't told my brother she blows me off."*

Amy was surprised to learn David knew Angel because he had never mentioned his family in their two months together. Angel went to the bathroom first, and Amy followed behind.

"Long time no see," Angel said.

"Same here," Amy replied.

Amy was terrified by Angel's next question.

"How did you come to know about my brother David?"

"Is David your brother? I did not know that you two were related."

"Now that you do, I need you to leave because if you don't, I'm going to

tell my brother about your entire life history. Do you honestly believe a man of his stature would want a lowlife trap like you?"

"Relax, Angel. It's not as if I'm attempting to marry him. I'm just having some fun with him, as men have done for years with women."

Angel grabbed Amy's neck and whispered. *"Bitch, if you don't dismiss my brother, you will be dead in twenty-four hours,"* which sent chills down Amy's spine because she still has nightmares about Dina's disappearance.

Amy continued to date David on the side, but she refused to attend family dinners. She was always making up excuses. David never questioned Amy. He just assumed she was a sickly person because she always had terrible headaches if it wasn't about her period.

But David wanted her to go to a football game with him, Dante, Angel, and her friends one time in particular. He had purchased the tickets a month in advance so that they could all travel together, but Amy became ill once more. She informed David that her son had chickenpox and that she couldn't leave him with the babysitter because she, too, had children. David understood because he and Dante had them before, so he agreed Amy needed to stay home with her son. But Amy despised the fact that Angel had her head in a vice grip hold knew she'll have Angel pay for ruining her happy moments with David.

Angel aimed at making Amy's life a living hell because Amy fled the house with her baby before she could kill her and take her child. In Angel's viewpoint, Amy cost her a hundred thousand dollars, and she knew Amy's child would be a hot commodity. Amy's son was mixed with black and Cherokee, and Angel had a couple who had the same bloodline and will pay the price agreed upon.

Angel found out where Amy stayed, and she had her house watched for weeks without her knowing it. What Amy didn't know was that the path of destruction was on its way. Angel planned to kidnap Amy's son and transport him to Washington, DC, but she didn't want to hurt her brother. That's why she had Killer have David pick up the packages this time. That way, David would be out of town when the kidnapping went down.

Amy was so afraid that she couldn't sleep at night. She knew once Angel saw her again, she would have hell to pay. But she didn't want David to know about her relationship or her involvement with Angel.

David left town two days later to pick up their packages. They didn't trust anyone other than themselves or Killer to carry out the trafficking runs.

David liked Amy a lot. However, he could tell something was wrong between Amy and his sister. David could tell the first time he took Amy to their house for dinner, but he let it go for the time being. He knew Amy was afraid of Angel because he held Amy's hand as they walked into the family dinner. Amy's palms sweat, and her face turned beet red as if she had seen a ghost. Everyone in the room could feel the tension. But David will soon find out why Amy feared his sister.

The saga continues. Stay tuned to David finding out about Angel kidnapping Amy's son.

Six

~

An Affair with Mike Trivet

Angel contacted her brothers for help to install a safe on her bedroom floor, but they were in a meeting with some bankers. She didn't want to disturb them, so she went to Mike's office instead. Angel needed to see Mike, anyway. She had been thinking about him a lot lately, and she was curious why.

Angel arrived at Mike's office and found him sitting behind his hand-crafted large mahogany desk. The man wore a custom-made navy blue Armani suit.

Angel pondered. *"Damn! I know he spent a lot of money on that suit, but I'm okay with it."*

Mike leaned back in his chair, asking Angel. *"What can I do for you today, pretty lady?"*

She asked Mike if he could recommend someone she could trust to install a built-in safe on her bedroom floor.

"Of course, I do. Me!" Mike stated.

"Stop playing, Mike. I needed someone who was both licensed and bonded." Angel said.

"I don't have those credentials, Angel, but I've learned how to install safes. So you think I went to law school solely to become a lawyer? I went to a

36

street school, girl. It's where I got credentials installing safes and working as a locksmith." Mike responded.

"Oh, you have jokes. I'll tell you what, funny man, come by my house tomorrow, bring the safe, and I'll be the judge of what you're capable of, okay?" Angel said, while staring at Mike.

Mike accepted Angel's invitation because he, too, had his sights set on her. Angel, however, had her own plans. She intended to chill some wine and serve herself as dessert.

Angel left Mike's office that day and went to Victoria's Secret to buy herself a nice and nasty nightgown. She also saw a hot pink number that she wanted, complete with a matching bra and pantyhose. She wanted her first experience to be memorable. Mike didn't know it's her first time, but he'd soon find out.

Mike arrived at Angel's house on time the next day with the safe. But, before ringing the doorbell, he smelled an aroma coming from the door.

"Damn! Something smells good. I'm curious what it is, and I'm hoping she invites me to dinner because a brother is always hungry." He thought to himself.

Angel, to his surprise, opened the door wearing nothing but a hot pink pantie and bra set from Victoria's Secret. In addition, she was wearing a pair of five-inch stilettos. Mike regarded Angel as if she were cotton candy on a stick, and he was prepared to devour her as if she were a steak with steak sauce.

Mike and Angel sat down to dinner, and for the main course, she directed Mike to the bedroom where she wanted her floor safe installed. When Mike opened Angel's bedroom door, she was naked, lying across her bed on a white mink blanket with red rose petals floating across it. He came close to passing out. Instead, Mike declared Angel to be the most beautiful woman he had ever seen. They slept together all night, and that was the start of their love affair.

Angel called her friends when Mike left Angel's house for work the next day. She had been ignoring them for the past three days, and they were curious about what she was hiding.

Angel had to get into the right frame of mind to tell Abby and Gabriel what was happening because she knew they were both looking at Mike. Angel, on the other hand, was lying back in the shadows, knowing she was going in for the kill. She was going to get Mike's attention without them, knowing she was having an affair with him behind their backs.

The relationship was becoming so intense that she felt compelled to let the cat out of the bag. Angel's plotting was clear to Abby and Gabriel, but they did not know she was so cunning. Angel didn't realize Mike had never asked her out to dinner or invited her to his apartment. She would have known Mike, the shiest attorney, was secretly seeing Gabriel if she had told them her intentions regarding the situation with Mike.

Angel invited Abby and Gabriel to lunch at her home. She instructed her chef to prepare smoked salmon, grilled vegetables, garlic bread sticks, and chill some mascots. Angel also mentioned that it was a lovely day and that she would like a table set up on a balcony.

When Abby and Gabrielle arrived at Angel's house at 1:30, they hugged as usual. They hadn't spoken in days. Then, with a glass of wine from the table, they all went up to the balcony. They sat at the table, said grace, and ate.

Abby started the conversation by telling about her new boyfriend. *"He was tall, dark, and handsome and a caterer by trade."* She said.

Angel and Gabriel were overjoyed for Abby because she was always complaining about being homesick. They wanted her to get out and meet new people. Gabriel was about to say something when her phone rang.

"Hold your horses, guys; this is my man," Gabriel stated.

Angel and Abby were shocked. They hadn't known she was seeing anyone since they arrived in Chicago, so even knowing she had a sidekick was a surprise. When Gabriel returned to the balcony, they began questioning her about her gentleman caller, but Mike had told Gabriel to keep their relationship private until he was ready to tell everyone, and she agreed. What Gabriel didn't realize was that Mike was regularly pounding Angel's brains out. Angel had yet to decide whether to tell the girls about her relationship with Mike, so she had made up a man for the time being. Angel informed Abby and Gabriel that she was seeing one of her brother's associates.

"Girl, you know the rules. Never mess around with your brothers' friends or associates." Abby exclaimed.

"Which of your brother's friends, was it Dante's or David's?" Gabrielle asked.

"Why?" Angel stated.

"I was simply inquiring," Gabriel responded.

But Gabriel was curious to know if it was Mike. Of course, Angel did not say it was Mike, but she also did not say it wasn't. So, to make a quick lie, Angel told them his name was Donovan, a man David had just hired as his right-hand man. Angel got away with her naughty ways for the time being, but her lies will catch up with her sooner than she thinks.

Soon after Abby and Gabriel had left, Mike called Angel. He had just invited Gabriel over to his house to watch a couple of movies with him, so he knew they were going. Gabriel was excited. She enjoyed being in Mike's company. He would set her soul on fire by performing lap dances and massages with warm oils.

Angel lay in bed that night, thinking about her sex session with Mike the night before. The tension was so intense that Angel reached for her nightstand drawer and pulled out her friend she called Big Mike. Angel lay in bed, sexing herself, while Mike was out on the town with her best friend, Gabriel.

Gabriel jumped in the shower after leaving Mike's apartment the next day. When Mike got out of the shower and dressed for work, he called Angel. He told her how much he missed her the night before, but he was exhausted and needed some rest.

When Mike got home from work, he asked Angel if she wanted any company. Angel told Mike she had many errands to run, but he could call her later that evening. *"Cool!"* Mike said, then they hang up.

A few minutes later, Mike's office door flew open, and in walked Abby, who was dressed in a trench coat with nothing underneath it.

Mike was a bad boy who was screwing all three of them, and they did not know. Mike asked Abby whether they believed her when she told them about her boyfriend. Abby informed Mike that they had.

"I don't enjoy lying to my friends, so why can't I tell them we've been dating since Angel's birthday party?" Abby asked.

Mike told Abby she couldn't tell anyone they were dating because it was against the rules to date friends or coworkers. Abby trusted Mike, so she was content for the time being. Abby looked at Mike and tossed her coat to the floor. They had sex on the desk, the floor, and even the windowsill in his office like rabbits in heat.

Mike had Angel, Abby, and Gabriel hooked on his ruse. He knew it would not last well, but his mind was racing with lies and desires to have them all. Mike also knew his plan was doomed. He was having unprotected sex with every one of them.

Mike admired the three girls' different complexion and wished for a daughter as beautiful as the three of them. His intention was to get them pregnant and have a daughter, then abandon them. However, he wasn't ready for a long-term commitment.

What Mike didn't realize was that they were both stunning and lethal, and he'd pay a high price if they ever discovered he was pitting them against each other.

Mike and his office secretary went out that night to prepare for a business meeting the next day. Looking over his shoulder that evening, he wasn't in Mike mode like he usually was. Angel wasn't feeling the lie Mike told her earlier, so she sat outside his office building and observed what was going on with him. She lit a Black & Mild and inhaled it while sitting in her car. Mike emerged from his office as Angel expelled the smoke from her lungs. He was with a beautiful woman, which irritated her, so she trailed close behind them. When he turned right, she turned right as well.

Angel was hot on Mike's tail when he and his female companion arrived at their destination. She requested a table in the back corner of the restaurant so she wouldn't be noticed. She almost fell out of her chair when she saw Mike reach over the table and kiss this woman. Angel thought to herself. Hold on there, Baby Girl. The ball is now in your court, and all you have to do is sit back and watch it happen, Baby Girl.

Angel was astounded when Baby Girl emerged from her mouth. She had a distinct memory of someone calling her Baby Girl. Angel was so up-set about her mind playing tricks on her. She almost forgot the reason she was there and why she was hiding. When she noticed Mike and his date exiting the restaurant, she followed them out two feet behind. Mike was still oblivious to Angel's presence behind them. Angel was right behind them, and if she had been a snake, she could have injected venom into both of them.

Mike dropped off his date at home continued on his way. As he drove into his parking lot, Angel waited the right moment so she can go home. Her mind was racing while on her way home. She thought she heard someone say Baby Girl, and she was terrified, eager to get home and get a glass of wine to calm her nerves.

Angel entered her house and ran down her long hallway to the bath-room. She had to use it because she had been holding her piss the entire time. Angel couldn't believe herself. *"Angel, you don't chase men. Men chase you".* She mused.

Mike called Angel's phone before she could get in the shower, asking if she wanted any company. Angel sneered before she could finish her sentence. *"Sorry, babe, I have company now. Can we meet tomorrow?"* She said.

Angel hung up the phone with Mike and went to bed alone, but she had a nightmare while sleeping. She hadn't had one since she was nine, but this time was different. She saw a man who resembled her brothers and herself.

"Baby Girl, you've grown into a stunning young lady. Don't be afraid. I'm your father. I love you and would do nothing to harm you." The man said.

Angel's nightmares were so frequent that she missed work because of insomnia, so she saw a therapist. Afraid, she went to see therapist Chloe Daniel, who said she would hypnotize her to solve her nightmares. Angel leaned back on the sofa as Ms. Daniel dangled her watch in front of her and told Angel to count to ten until she slept.

Angel sank into a deep sleep and moaned. She didn't want to see it.

Angel saw her mother murdered. She saw Tony smack her mother with a hammer. Angel didn't know Tony, but she knew Killer. She also remembered entering a big house with electric gates and being handed off to an old man with cigar breath.

Angel was assigned to a nanny that night to dress her for bed. The following day, she awoke to a beautiful woman in her room, Rakia, who claimed to be her mother. She was also told to have two brothers named David and Dante. She met them at breakfast and fell in love with them.

Angel awoke from hypnosis, fully awaken. Ms. Daniel did not know she had just created a monster. Angel would never forget what had happened to her mother. Angel thanked Ms. Daniel and agreed to meet again in two weeks.

Angel went into hiding after her therapist visit. She needed time to think. Angel came out of hiding after a month and returned to her grind, tougher than ever. She called Killer for a hundred kilos of cocaine and two pounds of heroin and flew to Hawaii to meet him. Angel wanted to look the guy in the eyes who killed her mother.

Mike and Angel's affair had come to a halt. She couldn't take on any more stress; she wanted to tell Mike his time was up, but she met with him one last time before dismissing him. Mike couldn't be trusted, but she wanted him to crack her back once more.

Angel waited two days before ending the affair and called Mike just to have sex. Mike wanted more and wanted to spend the night with her, but she refused. She told him that their experience was pleasant, but she needed to move on.

Angel hoped Mike would understand because if he didn't, she would put two in his head for thinking she was stupid.

Seven

∽

Angel On The Grind

Angel and her brothers arrived in Chicago and took over the city. The other drug dealers were curious about who they were. Some of them only knew Dante and David by association with Cane, and they feared them because they showed no fear and meant business.

Angel had gathered her forces and was ready to go into battle. They were stationed at each of her two properties as they surrounded her. The buildings were full of drugs, and the first floor was devoted to collecting and counting money.

She had at least five people working in the money machine, counting cash. The most challenging part was doing it completely naked. Angel had a distrust for everyone, and she made that clear to her troops. They needed to gain her confidence, which will not be easy.

On the second floor, they prepared drugs, bottled them, and dispensed them to her men.

The third floor was a crap house where she had card games, crap tables, pool tables, and even casino slot machines. At least ten soldiers guard the third floor because it averaged $10,000-$20,000 per night. Angel was raking it in. Her men who were selling drugs on the streets made her $40,000 per week.

Angel was so focused on getting things done that she almost forgot about the private investigator, Deacon Hayes. Angel called him and discovered that he had just returned to town. Her target, Killer Perez, was staying in a hotel in San Diego, California. He had been hiding there for the past two weeks. Deacon informed Angel that Perez would be out of money soon, so she needed to fly to San Diego to get things done before Perez disappeared again.

Angel took Deacon's advice and prepared to fly that night, but she couldn't leave town without backup. So she brought two of her soldiers with her: Tin Tin and Pop Eye, along with their two chicks. They were insane; one night at the zoo, they popped a gorilla's head off for throwing shit on them.

It took Angel and her soldiers two hours to fly from Chicago to San Diego. They rented an Impala and drove to the Imperial Drive hotel, room 212, where Deacon claimed Killer Perez stayed. They couldn't find him in his room. Perez had left the room to get something to eat. When Perez returned, he didn't notice he had company until he turned the lights on. Perez reached for his gun, but he was too slow. Tin Tin pointed her 9mm at his head, so he dropped his gun and asked what was up.

Angel looked at Perez, and he scared the shit out of her. He had scars all over his face, and it appeared as if someone had tried to cut his throat. Angel gathered herself to explain to Perez why she had come to San Diego. She told him she was in search of a killer for her crew. Perez thought she was insane and did not know he was a murderer.

Angel seemed to calm down Perez. Especially after she explained what she expected and how much he would earn. Perez was so focused on the paper he would make that he didn't notice Angel would be all over him like flies on shit.

As planned, Angel and her soldiers returned to Chicago with Perez but still wanted her soldiers to keep a close eye on him. Angel went to her other building, where she had set up the first floor for pregnant teenagers. She had about twelve girls staying there, and she spent a lot of money keeping them fed and clothed.

Angel put in a lot of time on the grind. She had a gang of female soldiers who robbed dope boys. They had mapped out the house of another drug dealer named St. Louis. He had a badass mansion with six bedrooms, three bathrooms, and two bodyguards stationed in front of it. The bedroom with a bed in the middle went down to the floor. There's a secret room beneath the floor that no one knew.

There were cameras and guns in the hidden room. St. Louis had enough guns in his fortress to start a war, even with Iraqi soldiers. So, for Angel soldiers to infiltrate St. Louis' place, they needed to work from the inside out. Angel assigned one of her female soldiers to be his maid, and she went through an agency, so there wasn't as much of a background check.

St. Louis went through four applications that day, and Mia fit the bill. Mia was in her forties, and she reminded him of his older sister Monique. He knew why, so Mia got a call from St. Louis that day, telling her to meet him at his house the next day at ten a.m., and had been told not to be late.

"Alright, we're in. The first time I saw him at Club Sexy, I knew he had some paper. Mike said he had ten million. If Mike's right, I'll give him a million dollars if no one from my team gets killed." Angel said to Mia.

Angel planned to feed St. Louis's arsenic a little at a time. They were going to do this robbery slowly and easily. She didn't want him dead just yet. What Angel didn't know game recognize game. When they saw St. Louis pepped Angel the night of her birthday party, St. Louis was only waiting until she finished what she had going on with Mike. St. Louis had been keeping a close eye on her because if he wanted her, he got what he wanted.

St. Louis had his right-hand man scoping out Angel the whole time. He wanted to make her his woman, but first, he tried to investigate her. He knew she wasn't from the Chicago area because he would have known everything he needed to know about her. That evening, St. Louis's right-hand man Richie reported to him that Angel was back in town. She had an army of soldiers ready for war, which put St. Louis in attack mode because everybody tried to get him.

St. Louis knew something was brewing, but he didn't know what, but he knew to keep his ear to the ground, and eventually, someone was going to snitch. So St. Louis thought he should go up to Club Sexy, where Angel's brothers hung out. Just maybe someone knew what was going on. Perhaps some of them, hoodrat bitches, knew what was about to pop off.

Angel had her female soldiers ready, but they had to wait for Mia to give them St. Louis's fortress map. Angel, Abby, and Gabriel went to Club Sexy the same night St. Louis was up there. He was in awe when he saw Angel walk through the door. *"Damn! That girl is more delicate than a thousand-dollar bottle of wine."* He said.

Angel and her girlfriends watched St. Louis's every move that night. Angel wanted to rob him, but something was pulling on her heartstrings about St. Louis too. He looked very enticing. She stalled, having second thoughts about robbing him. She thought to herself. Hell, I can make him mine and get his money that way. Angel's mind was all over the place. In her mind, they would take his fortune and laugh in his face after.

What Angel didn't know was St. Louis wanted her mind, body, and soul. She could have every dime he had because every time he saw Angel, it made his heart skip a beat; she had that kind of control over him, and she didn't even know it.

St. Louis found out a week later about Angel's history. He found out that Cane, the Hawaiian kingpin, was her father and Gloria Black, a.k.a. Glow was her mother. St. Louis also knew Tony was the one who killed her mother, but he didn't want to use this information he found out about Angel to hurt her unless he had to.

A month went by, and Angel told her female soldiers they had all the information they needed on St. Louis, so it was time to make a move. They were to go through an underground tunnel; this would put them precisely under his bed in the middle of the room. St. Louis had a button; they could push on the side of the wall to slide the bed back. The safe holding the money was inside the fish tank, underneath it. No one knew that but St. Louis and the guy who designed it, and to this day, the guy that designed it doesn't breathe anymore.

Angel and her soldiers were all geared up with their army fatigues and bulletproof vests and were ready to enter St. Louis's fortress that night. They knew he wasn't there because Mia had called and said he was gone out to dinner with his female friend, but he was due back in two hours. So while St. Louis was out at dinner, Angel and her female soldiers were making their way through the tunnel. They had enough explosives to blow St. Louis's house off the map. Still, before they could set the explosive in the position on the wall, they heard the alarm system say *front door open*. They almost shitted because they all had on watches and their timers set for two hours, but he made it back in an hour and a half.

Angel knew when to regroup and make their next move, a careful one. So they left St. Louis's house undetected, which blew Angel's mind when St. Louis came back from his date that early: either his date wasn't worth his time, or she was a boring chick. But frankly, Angel didn't give a damn. She just wished that the babe had enough stamina to keep the old boy happy for at least two hours damn.

Angel and her crew made it out of the tunnel undetected and safely made it back to their destination. But she was pissed because they were so close to getting those millions she could taste it. Angel felt like St. Louis knew they would hit his spot only if Angel knew the truth.

Mia got the job of being her soldier through St. Louis. He put her in Angel's fold to investigate her for him. She was St. Louis's younger sister Mecca a.k.a. Mia.

Mia had warned her brother of what was to come, so he cut his dinner short. St. Louis had to stop Angel from stealing from him, or he would have to kill her. His method of killing Angel would be to cut out her uterus and hang her ass from a flagpole in front of the police station for the entire world to see. St. Louis didn't want that. He had other plans for Angel.

St. Louis loved her gangsterism, but he just wanted her to be on his team. He knew she had potential, and that made his dick hard. Plus, she was beautiful and had her own money that was more than a plus for St. Louis.

Angel had struck nerves in St. Louis. He didn't even know it existed, but he had to figure out how to control Angel. Angel also had a thing for St. Louis, keeping him going in more ways than one. He had a body like a goddess and swagger that couldn't quit. Being only twenty-three,

Angel had more maturity than a woman in her forties, so she was about her business. Angel thought about forgetting about robbing St. Louis for now. Her black market baby-selling enterprise was failing because the girls weren't having their babies fast enough. So Angel went another route. She talked to Mike about opening up a stripper club. *Why not? There are so many pretty women around here who would welcome your club with honors. All you have to do is find a spot and come up with a name.* Mike said.

Angel was sitting at home, thinking, when the phrase "*Sugar Daddies*" came to her mind. Mike loved it, and he had already found her a spot five blocks from Club Sexy, and it was on and popping because Club Sexy had no competition.

She had ten strippers interview for the jobs, and Angel was surprised by their insaneness. Angel had one applicant sit on a beer bottle and suction it up her vagina. The other girl's snake licked her kitty cat like a cocaine blow pop. They were disgusting, but they could work on dancing poles, so Angel hired all ten girls to make money. That's it. If those bitches didn't have no respect for themselves, she sure didn't.

Eight

႟

Dante and David

Dante and David were on their grind as well. Their building was out of this world and their drug houses were exclusive.

They only played with the bigwigs, like politicians, lawyers, congressmen, judges, and even had high-priced call girls servicing their gentlemen callers.

Their building got high on the first floor, sexed on the second floor, and had a camera crew set up on the third floor for the blackmailing scam they were running for the married men with a lot to lose. They had photos and videotapes of every building activity.

They had a video of one judge freaking out with a pit bull, and a congressman dressed in drag and got screwed in the butt by a big black guy. Dante thought it was a bad idea, but it brought in cash, so he didn't mind.

Can I have that Chinese lady? The lawyer inquired.

Yes, if the price is reasonable, Dante responded.

What is the cost? The lawyer asked.

A thousand dollars for the round-trip fare. If you're unfamiliar with the term "round-trip," it refers to everything: pass, go, and beyond. Dante replied.

Then Dante and David sent the lawyer they called Dirty Old Man to the bathroom to ask the Chinese girl to stick her six-inch pumps up his arse. Then he wanted her to heel on his family jewels.

They'd seen some sick stuff, but this was out of bounds. They knew they needed to number and date their tapes to get paid.

Dante and David had opened a 24-hour restaurant. They were making a fortune, and they even opened two clothing stores, one for women only, called Bottoms Up. The other was unisex, with jewelry and everything and crazy handbags for women. They also had a princess lounge inside with musclemen waiting on women who entered, knowing their sizes.

Dante had finally met a woman. He had put his love life on hold while building his business. Now that everything is going according to plan, he can relax. He met Abigail two weeks ago, but never thought to call her.

He was walking into the grocery store when he accidentally bumped into her with his basket. He turned around and apologized, but was shocked when he saw it was Abigail Dawson. Abigail was stunning. To ask her out for lunch was too nerve-wracking for Dante. *"Man, get a grip,* he thought. *She is gorgeous, but she's human, too. Just ask her. What else can she say? Yes or no, end of the story."*

Dante gathered his courage and invited Abigail out to lunch, which she accepted. They went to his restaurant, The Sugar Shack.

While Dante was on his date with Abigail, David was having sex with Amy across town. He still had told no one, especially his sister, that he and Amy were still dating. David was still curious why Amy and Angel hated each other. What David didn't realize was that he'd find out soon because Amy's son, Conner, was about to go missing.

Amy inquired about David's plans for the evening.

Let me see. He replied.

David went out for the night, assuming Amy wouldn't want to, but he asked anyway. Amy decided to come over and sit with Conner. She agreed to go out, but she had to call the babysitter first.

Angel was sitting down the street with her crew when David and Amy left that evening. She almost choked when she saw David walk out the door with Amy because she had warned Amy to dismiss her brother, and she didn't. Angel couldn't believe Amy had lied to her about seeing

David. So, Angel reasoned to herself. *"Maybe if I kidnap her son, she won't want to play with me anymore."*

Angel had Abby and Gabriel put heroin in a needle so she could give the babysitter a shot that would only knock her out long enough to kidnap Conner. They slipped out Amy's back door unnoticed. The babysitter was asleep on the couch when they entered, so she didn't notice.

Gabriel shot the babysitter with heroin. As the babysitter was out, they went to Conner's room, where he was fast asleep. Angel took Conner and led him down the hall. Angel left a note at Amy's house saying, *"Bitch, I told you not to play with me."*

When David and Amy returned to her apartment, she noticed her babysitter nodding in and out of consciousness.

What in the world is going on? What's the matter with you, Shelly? Amy stated.

Shelly was speechless. She told Amy she was dizzy and didn't know why. Amy dashed down the hall to check on Conner. She panicked when she couldn't find Conner in his room and screamed. David ran fast down the hall that he almost fell. All Amy could do was cry.

Not my son! He's all I have. Please! Find my son, please. He cried to David.

David felt so bad. He called in some favors because he believed that kidnapping was in the house, and if it was heads, they're going to roll for this one. David also contacted Dante for help. He put Hammer on the job, knowing he was a retired police officer. He wanted the best, and time was an issue as well. Conner was born with a heart condition and needed to take heart medicine once a day.

Amy could not sleep. Conner had been gone for over 48 hours. He'd already missed two shots, and she was terrified for her son. David went to Amy's house to tell her the results of his search for Conner, which he hadn't found yet.

In her premonition, Amy knew who kidnapped her son, and she had to take her chances telling David, hoping he would understand. If David didn't, it was his loss because that was her past.

Amy told David every detail about her and Angel, including the video of Angel killing Dina and her black-market baby-selling business. David was shocked to learn Angel was in the baby-selling business. He knew they were in some trouble, but babies weren't an option. He couldn't believe his ears.

Let me get back to you. I need to clear my mind. If I hear anything about your son, I will contact you as soon as possible. I will call all right. David told Amy.

David was so shaken by Amy's sudden revelation that he called Dante to meet him at their restaurant as soon as possible. He was so disturbed by their sister killing pregnant teens and stealing their children that he despised Angel.

David looked devastated when Dante arrived at his brother's location.

Man, you look like you've seen a ghost. Inform your brother of the situation. Dante said.

They were never taught to harm children when they were growing up. Their mother, as well as their grandfather, were adamantly opposed. They were ruthless, but children were never involved in the murders they committed.

When David told Dante what was going on with Amy involving Angel, Dante was devastated. They were looking at Angel in a different light now. Their little sister had sold her soul to the devil. Angel grew up in the same house as them, so they were curious about what happened to her. They were all in Chicago to make money, but Sister Girl took it to another level. Angel had become scandalous, and she had also gone too far. She was causing trouble for someone close to David. He would not let her get away with kidnapping Conner. David wasn't sure if it was her, but he was on the verge of finding out.

David was on his way to one of Angel's apartment buildings, where Hammer and Dante were waiting for him when Dante called him. Hammer told Dante and David he saw a Cherokee couple entered Angel's building with a bag and a big teddy bear, but they hadn't come out yet, so they parked outside to see what was up.

Ten minutes later, the couple emerged from the building, carrying Conner, and the shit hit the fan. The couple did not know why Hammer had a gun pointed at their heads. David took Conner from the couple's arms and walked to his car to return Conner to his mother. After leaving Amy's house, he called Dante and told him they needed to have a serious talk with Angel.

Angel was pissed as she watched what was happening outside her apartment building. Her brothers and Hammer were taking $200,000 from her. She knew well that this was going to be a war. Dante and David had set the stage for World War III to erupt in the Windy City of Chicago.

Nine

～

The Love Connection

Angel was sitting in her apartment window when she noticed a vintage white Cadillac from the 1920s passing by. Angel had seen the Cadillac before, but it no longer bothered her. The car passed her apartment so frequently, which raised her suspicions as its tinted windows. She couldn't see the driver inside because it was dark, but she wanted to know who was driving it. Angel didn't know that the man driving the white Cadillac past her house every night was her dream hunter.

Angel was so in tune with St. Louis it drove her crazy. He had power, but he damn ran through her mind like blood running through her veins. *"Maybe I should meet with him to find out what's up."* She mused.

Angel went to Club Sexy alone that night, hoping to meet St. Louis with no one knowing. She needed to understand why he had her heart racing and why he was always on her mind. Angel arrived at 8:30 p.m. St. Louis wasn't there, so she sat at the bar and had a couple drinks.

Eric, the bartender, asked her. *Did you know anyone by the name of Gloria Black, a.k.a. Glow?*

"I didn't know her," Angel replied.

"You and she could be twins. I swear you guys could be twin sisters." Eric stated.

Angel had two drinks and was about to leave when she noticed St. Louis walked in.

"Let me get another apple martini, please." She said to Eric.

Angel took her drink from Eric and turned away as if she hadn't seen her dream man enter. Angel was thrilled to see St. Louis that her panties got wet just looking at him. She pretended to be with another groupie and sat at the bar drinking until St. Louis noticed her alone at the bar. St. Louis approached the bar and ordered a Crown Royal with water. *"Damn! This man smells like a million dollars."* She thought.

St. Louis sat for an hour watching Angel before getting up and making the first move. He felt his heartstrings pull in his chest, just as Angel felt that night. Then he stood up and approached Angel. He introduced himself as Ronald Louis, a.k.a. St. Louis.

"Hello, my name is Angel Salvador. It's great to finally meet you." Angel said.

St. Louis was so taken with Angel that he had to inquire about her ethnicity. Angel informed him she was Hawaiian and Black.

Little mama, you're a very sexy woman, and now that we're alone, can I take you to dinner? He asked.

Of course you can, but only if I choose the restaurant, Angel replied.

Cool. Or I can take you to my spot and have my chef prepare a meal for us. He said.

Let's go to your spot then, Angel said.

St. Louis called his home phone before leaving Club Sexy to make sure Mia was in her room. No one answered, so he called Mia on her cell. She was working for Angel, so he could take her there. St. Louis vowed to tell Angel how he had secured his cradle, and it would be difficult to enter his fortress.

When they arrived at his place, St. Louis went into the kitchen to get them a bottle of wine to enjoy before dinner. He would tell Angel about her attempt to rob his fortress, but he had to be careful with his words. He didn't want to scare her away before their love connection had even begun.

Angel wasn't sure what would happen between her and St. Louis, but she had a feeling. He took her hand, and she felt butterflies in her stomach. St. Louis waited until dinner was served before he blew up Angel. He wanted her to feel at ease first. Angel felt comfortable with St. Louis. She had her shoes taken off when St. Louis returned. Women don't take their shoes off in a man's house unless they feel safe doing so. After dinner, St. Louis thought it was time to warn Angel about the consequences of robbing his fortress.

St. Louis dismissed the chef and sat with Angel by the fire in the den. St. Louis sat across from Angel, holding her hand and looking deep into her eyes. She got nervous and sweated. Angel lowered her head so she wouldn't have to look St. Louis in his big brown eyes.

St. Louis took his hand and raised Angel's chin to his face, then said, *"Why are you so nervous? We must first become friends before we can connect on an emotional level."*

Angel was initially quiet, sensing St. Louis was being sincere. It wasn't deception, so she was open to hearing what he had to say. However, Angel's body shivered at what he said next.

"Angel, first and foremost, I want you to know that I adore you, and I love your gangsta style. But a gangster-like me puts niggers to sleep, and you were on the verge of crossing the line when you and your soldiers planned to rob my fortress." He said.

St. Louis spit that out of his mouth, and Angel looked embarrassed. Angel was stunned and wanted to leave because she thought it was a ruse.

Angel calmed down a little after realizing it wasn't a set-up. She thought to herself, *"This man must really like me or something because if I had a gangster in my camp planning to rob me, that person would swim with the fishes."*

On the other hand, Angel knew she had to find the snitch in her camp or someone would die.

Angel and St. Louis talked for hours, and a relationship began that night. Angel desired to make love to St. Louis, but St. Louis preferred to get to know Angel first. He had girls lined up to have sex with him, so he could have it whenever he wanted. But all he wanted was Angel.

Angel spent the entire night at St. Louis' house. The chef returned the following morning to prepare their breakfast. After eating, St. Louis took Angel back to Club Sexy, where she had left her car. Angel noticed a white Cadillac in his garage before they went. It was the same car she had seen drive past her apartment several times. *"Oh, he's a stalker as well."* She thought. But it wasn't because St. Louis being a stalker. He was only monitoring his investment.

Angel didn't know her brothers would be in her car when dropped off at Club Sexy. They tried calling Angel, but she sent them all to voicemail. Angel knew what they wanted, and she knew their meeting wouldn't go well after the way they treated her. Dante was the first to approach Angel.

"You realize you've gone too far, don't you? You've taken money-making to a whole new level, and we believe you should step down." Dante said.

"Are you two punks insane? I was sent here to get paid just like the two of you, and if yawl doesn't back down from me, there will be real consequences." Angel shouted.

David was so upset he reached over the seat and slapped Angel. Dante snatched Angel's gun from her purse as she tried getting it to shoot David.

"Have you gone insane? Have your hustling gotten you so far that you're willing to kill your own brother?" Dante shouted.

Angel looked at Dante with bloodshot eyes.

"We being related? Don't live here anymore. You two half-breed motherfuckers have just started a war." Angel exclaimed.

Angel awoke the next day, hoping she was dreaming, but she wasn't. She still had the slap mark on her face from David. She couldn't get over the fact that her brother had put his hands on her, and she was determined that he would never disrespect her again. David and Dante had to be dealt with right away.

Angel was thinking about her brothers when the phone rang, interrupting her thoughts. It was St. Louis. He wanted to have dinner with her. The butterflies in her stomach fluttered again upon hearing his voice. *"I need to get closer to this man so I can get deep into his heart."* Angel reasoned.

"Where do you want to eat?" Angel inquired.

"Wherever you like to dine, sweetie," he said.

Angel and St. Louis had dinner at an Italian restaurant of her choosing. They had a great time together until St. Louis noticed the slap mark on her face. He was furious.

"Who put their hands on you?" he inquired of Angel."

"Don't be concerned. I'm fine." She stated.

"I know you can, but that's why I'm here: to protect and serve my lady." He said.

"Excuse me. I didn't realize you were my man." Angel said.

"Well, now you know, sweetness. So, what's the deal?" St. Louis asked.

Angel was overjoyed St. Louis chose her. Angel loved being St. Louis' woman, but she had to tell Abby and Gabriel. Her girls needed to know what she'd been up to. They arrived at Angel's apartment at ten-thirty. They ate breakfast and talked about what Angel had been up to. Angel told her best friends she had secured St. Louis. Abby and Gabriel were shocked, as it was the man they attempted to rob. *What was she thinking? Or did she fall and hit her damn head?*

Angel had to break down and confess she had feelings for St. Louis, despite them having attempted to rob him just a week ago.

"Our girl has gone insane. Do you know what the man would do if he discovered we were only two seconds away from robbing him when he returned home early?" Abby said to Gabriel.

"Angel, sweetheart, do you realize the power this man possesses? He could murder us, bury our assess, and no one would know. What were you thinking, Angel? Are you so caught up with your feelings that you didn't notice he's taking advantage of you, girl?" Gabriel asked.

Angel was so disappointed with her friends' reactions to her new-found relationship. Finally, she told them to leave her house and return home because she didn't need them anymore. They were frustrated because Angel had flipped out on them. She was changing, and not for the better. She was going insane, and they were seriously worried about her.

Angel did not know that St. Louis had tracked down the person who slapped her despite her silence. So he set to find out who put that hand mark on his beautiful woman's face. St. Louis didn't care, even if it was her brother. He wanted vengeance and would get it. As a result, St. Louis had his right-hand man set up shop outside of David and Dante's restaurant so he could talk to them about Angel's well-being. If they wouldn't, they could settle the score by exchanging gunfire. For him, no one would touch Angel as long as he was her man, family member, or not.

One night, Angel ran into Gabriel and Mike, hugging and kissing as they exited the theater. She was surprised to see Gabriel hugging her ex-man, so she approached them.

"What the hell are you doing?" Angel asked Gabriel.

"Mike and I have been together for a while," Gabriel explained.

"Oh, snap! So, Mike, did you tell Gabriel that you and I had been kicking for a while as well?" Angel exclaimed.

Mike was at a loss for words, but he knew this would come back to bite him in the arse one day. Mike knew the situation would deteriorate further if Abby found out, so he decided to lay it all on the table.

Mike informed Angel and Gabriel that he had seen them on the low at different times. He wanted to try the flavor of the month because they were all so lovely, and they all tasted very sweet to him. Angel shot Mike in the chest before he could finish his sentence.

Angel spit in Mike's face as he fell to the ground and said, *"I hope your punk-ass die bastard like the dog you are."*

Angel looked up at Gabriel, who was standing in a daze. Angel stated. *"Snap out of it, bitch, and you better be gone by daylight tomorrow, or I'm going to smoke your ass as well for being so inconsiderate."*

Angel and Gabriel called Abby the same night, but neither received an answer. Finally, Angel left Abby a message telling her she knew about her fling with Mike, so if she valued her life, she better leave. If not, she would be in the hospital, lying beside Mike, fighting for his life. That was all Abby needed to hear. She couldn't take any chances. Abby needed to get the hell out of dodge because she knew if Angel got angry, she'd kill her own mother, so she had to put some distance between them.

That was the end of Angel's friendship with Abby and Gabriel until she had to break down and ask for help because she was truly stuck.

Ten

〰

Uprooting the Devil

Angel had become so engrossed in her relationship with St. Louis that she had neglected her work. So she told Louis, *I love being with you, baby, but I have to go back to work.* St. Louis was happy that Angel knew her priorities, so he didn't argue with her about leaving him for the day. He liked it when a woman got down to business, so he welcomed it.

The following day, after leaving St. Louis, Angel woke up early and went straight to her dope house. She discovered she had been duped for a hundred thousand dollars by one of her female soldiers. Angel wanted to make an example of her. So she dispatched her other soldier, Shaky, to bring Gallia to her office. When Shaky and Gallia arrived at her office, Angel grabbed Gallia's hair and yanked her to the ground. Then, Angel took out her gun and placed it in her mouth, saying, *I'm going to ask you one time, bitch, where is my money?*

Gallia was so terrified that she pissed on herself. *I'm sorry, I'll repay you. I promised my kids to buy some items they needed, and I had to pay my rent.* Gallia begged Angel.

I don't give a flying fuck because I pay you a thousand dollars per week, bitch. You had absolutely no reason to steal from me. Angel shouted in anger.

Angel paraded Gallia through the lobby for the soldiers to see what happens if they steal from her. She had wrapped her neck with a tape, and her 45-caliber pistol against her temple. Angel blew Gallia's brains out in front of everyone. The scene scared the soldiers, except those men who knew how heartless bitch she was.

Gallia was dead and Angel's people could not mention her name. Her mother became concerned when Gallia didn't go home that night. Gallia regularly checked up on her children, so she thought something terrible might have happened. Gallia's mother went to the compound, but she didn't see Gallia. She asked Keys, one of the female soldiers, if she had seen her daughter. *No, not today, but if I see her, I'll tell her you stopped by,* Keys replied.

Keys knew Gallia's mother would never see her daughter again since she was dead. Keys wishes she had someone to come and check on her because she knew it's only a matter of time before Angel turns on her.

Angel hadn't seen St. Louis in two days. They talk every day, but they had spent no time together, so she called him and asked if she could come by and hang out, and he said yes.

When she arrived, St. Louis was waiting for her outside with outstretched arms, ready to welcome her. When Angel walked through the door, he immediately got a label designer to size her up. St. Louis would attend a wedding, and he wanted Angel to come along with him as his date. Angel was happy that her man would take her out in public because they had previously remained hidden in his home. They had only gone out as a couple once, and attending a wedding together would be wonderful.

Angel was having fun at the wedding when someone snatched her arm and said, *What the hell are you doing here with this nigger?*

Angel turned around to see Dante in his rear form. He was so mad that he foamed at the mouth like a pit bull.

Brother man, if you don't let go of my arm, I'm going to drop you where you stand, Angel said.

All hell broke loose before Angel could reach for her purse. St. Louis' bodyguards and Dante's right-hand man started fighting, and before she knew it, all of Dante's undercover men were shooting. The guests at the wedding were dropping like flies. St. Louis was even hit in the shoulder. Luckily, he was unharmed.

Angel apologized to St. Louis for his brother spoiling his best friend's wedding and promised to make amends when they returned home. He smiled because he knew she meant it. When Angel and St. Louis returned to his apartment, he had already called the doctor to remove the bullet from his shoulder.

That night, St. Louis decided it was time to wake Angel up from her stupor. He wanted her to see the Salvador family's true colors. First, they killed both her parents, and David and Dante were her brothers from a different mother. She was born in Chicago and was kidnapped by Mr. Salvador's right-hand man, Killer when she was five years old.

St. Louis began telling Angel about her alleged mafia family. He had documents to back up everything he said. He had images of Cane, the Hawaiian kingpin, and Gloria Black, her mother. Angel's mother, which she couldn't recall until her therapist brought them back, owned Club Sexy before she was murdered. Her father called her Baby Girl.

"Hold on, St. Louis, this is a lot of information. Please allow me a moment to think. What happened to my father, the kingpin, if you know all of this?" Angel asked.

"Baby, the grandfather you thought, Mr. Salvador and his bodyguards, including Killer, had your father killed. They invited him to Hawaii to spend time with their family before murdering him in the house you grew up in," he said.

Angel was so angry. She cried so hard that her nose bled.

Angel looked at St. Louis and said, *everyone with the Salvador surname will perish, including my brothers and that lying ass bitch Rakia a.k.a. Mommy, dearest. She'll wish she'd never met Angel Carter. Thank you for telling me who I really am. Living in that family, I always felt out of place. Now I understand why. I was not born to Rakia Salvador, but to Gloria Black. She never mistreated me, but I never felt a mother-daughter love that comes with having a child.*

Angel was out for vengeance on the Salvadors, and she craved them like a piranha. She called her grandfather to spend a few days with them. She aims to kill everyone in the house in two days. Angel called the airlines to book a Saturday departure. She also contacted St. Louis to let him know she was returning home for a few days. Still, St. Louis knew something was up because Angel's voice wasn't as sweet and sensual as usual.

The next day, Angel was off to Hawaii. Killer was going to meet her at the airport. She was only hoping to keep her calm. It was revenge for what they had done to her parents. This would be a killing that would be spoken about for years. When Angel's plane landed six hours later, Killer was waiting for him. No one knew that their little princess was on a killing mission; it wasn't societal but personal.

Angel was received with kisses and hugs by the Salvador family. Rakia cradled Angel like an infant, and Angel resented it. Angel couldn't wait till bedtime because she had planned her demise on the aircraft. After supper, the family had drinks by the pool. Then they went to the cinema room, which was set up like a movie theater. Finally, Mr. Salvador excused himself from everyone and went to his office at the back of the house.

Angel decided it was the best time to talk to her grandfather. But, unfortunately, she'd already tainted his drink. *"He should have been nodding off by now,"* she reasoned.

Angel went to her grandfather's office, and he was nodding so loudly that he didn't notice Angel going through his wall safe. Taking all the money and information she needed about what happened to her parents. Mr. Salvador was a sick man. He had just been diagnosed with lung cancer and had been given two months to live, but he didn't want his family to know.

Angel tied her grandfather to a chair and slapped him to wake him up. When she did, she said, *wake up, I have a couple of questions for you, old man, before I kill you.*

Angel recalled her childhood memories as she asked her grandfather questions. She remembered Killer and the other bodyguards discussing how they killed Cane. They let the pit bulls eat his family jewels and made him die slowly and painfully.

Angel refocused her thoughts and began telling her grandfather that she knew he was the one who ordered the hit on her parents. She also knew he wasn't her real grandfather, and his bitch daughter wasn't her actual mother, and Killer helped in the murder of her mother and her kidnapping. Mr. Salvador was horrified but unable to call for help. Angel had two needles ready for Mr. Salvador. But first, she cut his balls off as he did to her father. She wanted him to feel the same agony.

Mr. Salvador collapsed after she cut his balls. Then Angel injected his neck with two battery acid needles. It was all set. Mr. Salvador vanished. Leaving her Mommy Dearest for last, Angel went down the hall to the cinema room, where Killer and the other bodyguards were asleep from the drugged drinks she had given them.

Angel went to get the rope from the utility room. She chained Killer and the bodyguards, then walked out to the pool to drain it and pour acid. Angel removed their eyeballs with an ice pick and served them to the pit bulls. Then she pulled them all and dumped them in the acid pool. Angel saved the best for last when she went to her Mommy Dearest.

Angel entered Rakia's bedroom, but she was sound asleep, so she did not disturb her. Instead, she pulled two pairs of handcuffs from her goodie bag and cuffed Rakia to the bedpost. Angel went out to the garage and got the gas can near the lawnmower. She stormed back into the house, intending to wake her up by beating the snot out of her, before confessing what she had done to her and murdering her parents. Angel despised Rakia so much that she whooped her; then, she turned around, took a pair of wire pliers, and pulled each of her teeth out while she was still conscious. Angel took the gasoline, poured it all over Rakia, lit a cigarette, thumped it on Rakia, and set her on fire when she passed out.

After the house caught fire, Angel went out into the yard and slaughtered the pit bulls. They were barking and jumping around the yard. Angel took her 38 caliber and blew their heads out. Angel stood with the rest of the people who were watching the fire down the street. Because she was disguised, no one noticed her.

She was back on a plane bound for Chicago the next day. Without her knowledge, St. Louis was hot on her tail. He had followed her to Hawaii.

He was only there as a backup if she needed him and would only be a phone call away.

When Angel landed in Chicago, the first person she called was St. Louis. She needed to get rid of some tension. Angel had finally gotten rid of some Salvadors. But she still had her brothers to deal with, and their time was running out.

St. Louis arrived at Angel's house on time. She hugged and kissed him passionately. St. Louis knew she had blood on her hands, so he knew she needed a release and was waiting for him. They slept together all night. St. Louis asked her if she wanted to talk about anything when they woke up the following day.

"No, not right now, but I want to talk about taking my brothers off this planet. If you want to discuss it, I'm all ears." She said.

Angel made plans to protect her brothers' properties. She wanted to take over all of their businesses before she killed them. But she had to put up a front with them and act as if she had changed, so she invited them over to lunch, which they both accepted because they wanted their little sister back. So Angel played the role of the little sister very well, and they both fell for her act.

Dante and David were having lunch with Angel when they received a phone call from Caruso's mafia kingpin. He informed them that their entire family had been murdered and needed to return home as soon as possible. They needed to make funeral arrangements, as well as figure out who would be so bold as to wipe out an entire mafia family in one night. Dante, David, and Angel were on the first plane home, and when they arrived, there wasn't a home to go home to, but Angel knew who killed everyone, including the dogs.

Dante was enraged, because there were no bodies to bury. Mr. Salvador had left everything for his three grandchildren, so they had to meet with the family lawyer for the will read. They had twenty million dollars to divide among the three of them. They almost choked when they heard the will reading of the money and the overseas account of a billion dollars, but they kept their cool.

After they received their checks from the lawyer, it was time to bounce. They returned to Chicago to devise a plan to find out what happened to their family. However, Angel faked the crying pan to convince her brothers that she felt the pain of their loved ones' deaths. If Dante and David had known, she would have died.

David and Dante had been on a rampage since their family's death. They were so mad that they began blackmailing their clients and didn't care who was hurt. Dante was driving around the city drunk one night when he hit an innocent bystander crossing the street and killed him, and he didn't even stop to see if the person was dead.

Angel began her plan the next day to put her brothers out of their misery. She knew they were aware of her will as well, but she didn't care if they left her anything because she had enough money to burn. So she requested her brothers meet her at Club Sexy that night.

Angel had figured out exactly how to get her brothers to meet her at Club Sexy. She informed them she had discovered who had murdered their family and that she would wait for them in her car. When David and Dante arrived, they noticed Angel's car and went over to it to get in. Both of them got in the back seat, but for Angel, nothing mattered anymore because both of them would die.

"Did you two know our grandfather ordered a hit on our father and that he had his eyeballs cut out and fed to the pit bulls?" Angel began.

Yes, we were there to see it happen, Dante and David said.

But they were both curious how she found out. They also informed Angel that her crackhead mother was a home-wrecker, and she was also dealt with.

Angel got so angry that she began shooting inside the car. She had forgotten that St. Louis was in her trunk. Angel pierced her brothers so many times that they resembled swiss cheese. She drove out of the parking lot as quickly as she could, then jumped out of her car and opened the trunk two blocks away from the club. She jumped for joy when she saw St. Louis' eyes open and that he wasn't hurt.

St. Louis and Angel drove her car to a remote location, removed the plates, and set fire to it. Angel's car was discovered two days later after she reported her brother missing. She also told the police that David had borrowed her car earlier in the day to avoid raising suspicions about her.

The cops told Angel that her brothers were severely burned that she wouldn't even need to have a funeral for them, but they will keep the case open until they find the murderer.

Eleven

❦

Who is Mike Trivet?

Mike had finally been released from the hospital. Still, before he did, a mail carrier delivered him an envelope sent by Mr. Salvador before his death and only to be given by his attorney if he died. Mike did not know who Mr. Salvador was until he opened the package and read his apology to the family who had given him up for adoption.

Mike was Cane's son from Mr. Salvador's maid. Mr. Salvador discovered Cane's affair with his maid, Rosa. He was so outraged for Cane having no respect for his daughter, so he kept Rosa on as the maid until she gave birth. When Rosa gave birth to a seven-pound-six-ounce boy, he made Rosa put the baby up for adoption. She was to never speak of having a baby unless she wanted to end up dead.

Cane did not know she had a child with Rosa, but he suspected something was wrong when he was assigned to run the family business in Chicago. Mr. Salvador, on the other hand, knew who had adopted the child. When his adoptive mother died, he continued to support his upbringing and sent money to his grandmother.

He also had pictures of every football game he had ever played in. He sent the photos along with the money he sent in the envelope delivered to the hospital. Mr. Salvador also displayed photographs of Angel, David, and Dante, along with a letter.

Dear Mike,

These are your brothers. Angel, this pretty little princess, is your sister by your father. All of you were born to different mothers, and I hope you can forgive me for taking your family away from you. If you are reading this letter, it means that I have moved on and that you may begin a relationship with your brothers and sisters.

Mr. Salvador

While Mike was trying to gather his thoughts, he saw breaking news on TV, including a report of Angel's car and the two bodies discovered inside. Angel was the first person who came to his mind. Angel had her name all over his brother's death. Mike had to get out of that hospital quickly because he knew from Abby, who was still in contact with him, that the entire Salvador family had been murdered, including the dogs. If Angel did that, he knew she would go after him next.

What Mike didn't know was that Angel had copies of every letter Mr. Salvador had sent him. She knew Mike was her brother, and Tony, Dante, and David were her brothers as well. Through Salvador's safe documents, she also discovered that Cane has a daughter somewhere out there. She was born at the same time as Angel. Angel is also looking for Cane's other daughter's mother, who is a social service worker in the Chicago area. Her name was written in the documents Angel took from Mr. Salvador's safe. Helen Davis was her name. She would find her sister if she went down to the social service department and find Helen Davis, but she didn't want Mike around at all. She wanted him dead as well. But Mike was smarter than his twin brothers. He also wanted Angel dead so he could start his own empire. Mike was released from the hospital and went to a hotel outside of town. He didn't want any of Angel's soldiers to notice him.

Mike had decided, and he needed to devise a plan to get Angel. He couldn't even return to his office because he knew Angel had his house and job under lockdown. Angel had her soldiers scouring the Chicago area for Mike. Angel knew he had been released from the hospital. Her soldiers didn't arrive at the hospital in time to retrieve Mike because he had left the hospital early.

The next day, Mike went to borrow a car from a friend to go look at Angel's apartment. Mike was determined to catch Angel, but he did not know she was wrapped around St. Louis like a python. So Mike decided to disguise himself as an old man and go hang out at Angel's club. He wanted to meet one of Angel's strippers. That way, he could get closer to Angel.

One night, Mike was sitting in Angel's club when Angel and St. Louis walked in. Mike thought to himself, *"Look at her; she looks like a million bucks, even though she's deranged as hell. That bitch wipes out a whole mafia family. So if it's the last thing I do, I'm going to make that bitch pay for killing our brothers."*

Angel and St. Louis became a lovely couple. They spent a significant amount of time together. That's why Mike couldn't catch her by himself just yet. That night, Mike followed Angel and St. Louis out of the club. They returned to St. Louis' house, and Mike thought to himself, *"I can kill two birds with one stone."* Mike didn't like St. Louis because he reminded him of himself.

Mike did not know his adoptive mother had a son when she was sixteen and placed him for adoption when she discovered she was pregnant. When she went into labor, she and her boyfriend went to a shady doctor, which scared her from ever having her own children. That's why she took in Mike. St. Louis, of course, reminded him of himself because they share a father.

Mike had been watching St. Louis' house all night, but he knew it wouldn't be easy to get to Angel as long as St. Louis was guarding her. So Mike decided to postpone his move until he could devise a better strategy. He wanted Angel so badly because she shot him, and now he found out she's his sister. *This is too much, and getting a call from Gabriel telling me she has my daughter is surreal.* Mike had always wanted a little princess, and now he was about to get one in six months.

Mike wanted to be present at his daughter's birth, so he had to bury Angel six feet deep. Mike didn't know that Angel had been watching his every move since the day he left the hospital. Her soldiers arrived late, but she and St. Louis were there on time. They were both aware of Mike's disguise and that he followed them to St. Louis' house. Angel and St. Louis were laying the groundwork for Mike to fall right into Angel's clutches.

Angel was throwing a party to celebrate the launch of her new business. It's a new club called Sexy Sophistication. You must be dressed to impress to enter Angel's new club, Sexy Sophistication. She even had a fifty-dollar cover charge, and after 10pm, the cover charge becomes sixty dollars. Mike was going to the celebration, and he had to be ready for anything. Unfortunately, Mike didn't realize that the night of Club Sophistication's opening, he wouldn't even make it out of his hotel room. St. Louis had a bodyguard stationed at the Ritz Hotel, where Mike was staying. He should have had enough sincerity to check into a dump.

Mike was in the shower when St. Louis's right-hand man snuck into Mike's room. He had some guitar wire to tie Mike until Angel arrived. Angel's plan was to show her face in Club Sexy Sophistication and sneak out long enough to kill Mike and return before anyone noticed she was gone.

Mike was tied up and bleeding in a chair when Angel arrived at the hotel.

"*Oh, what a tangled web we weave!*" Angel said.

"*Bitch, you can kill me, but I'll see you in hell one day,*" Mike told Angel.

Angel wrapped a guitar wire around Mike's penis until it snapped. Mike's eyes rolled around in his head as he bled. Then Angel turned to face Mike and said, "*Don't pass out right now, dear brother. I'm not done yet.*"

What Angel did next knocked Mike out cold. She had St. Louis' right-hand man screw Mike in the ass. After that brief session, Angel took a machete and cut Mike's head. They put the rest of Mike's body in a plastic bag and delivered it to the police station.

The front desk officer at the station discovered a bag on his desk, immediately opened it and threw it away. It was a dreadful experience. The entire team was on a mission to find out who would be so bold as to behead well-known Chicago attorney Mike Trivet.

Mike Trivet's case was widely publicized around the world. Posters with his face were all over the news. When Angel woke up the following day, the news was on, and when she saw Mike's face, she became irritated again. She even spits on the screen of the television. Angel thought to herself, *"I should have burned him alive just for disrespecting my friends and me."*

Gabriel experienced abdominal pains after hearing the news. She couldn't believe her eyes when she saw it. Gabriel just talked to Mike about their daughter and baby names an hour ago, and it didn't sit well with her. She knew Angel had something to do with her unborn child's father's death. Gabriel also knew Angel had taken out her own mafia family, the Salvador's. Gabriel's father was also the head of a mafia organization. She needed to return to Hawaii to meet with him. Angel had to be stopped by any means necessary. Angel had transformed into the devil and had to be stopped.

Gabriel arrived home just in time. Her father was about to leave for a trip, but Gabriel wanted him to know that Angel had killed his best friend, Mr. Salvador, as well as Dante and David and the father of her unborn child. Gabriel's father was rendered speechless. He was curious why she believed Angel was to blame for the death of her own family.

Mike had just discovered that the Salvador's were not Angel's biological family. Cane was her father, and that Mr. Salvador was the one who ordered the hit on both of her parents. Gabriel informed her father that Angel had threatened her because they were both into the same guy, and she also threatened Abby.

Gabriel's father assured her he would put some people on Angel's side. He had some Russian hitmen who owed him a favor and would love to burn Angel's ass. Gabriel's father called in his favor before he left for his trip, and they were delighted to go in search of some fresh meat.

Angel was content to be alone in the world without a family until she met St. Louis and moved in with him so he could monitor her. Unfortunately, St. Louis didn't realize that when the Russians came looking for

Angel, they would kill everyone in the house to get to the people they wanted. Gabriel had given her father all the information he needed to find Angel, including her clubs and the six buildings she was now in charge of. So the Russians set up camp in Chicago, even renting a black Tahoe with Chicago plates to avoid suspicion. They were there to leave a trail of destruction in their wake.

Angel was going to pay. Gabriel despised Angel and demanded that she pay for Mike's death. She even considered becoming her friend again just to get close enough to her to cut her throat. Angel had forgotten entirely about her friends, Gabriel and Abby. They were once best friends, but now they were on Angel's shitlist, and Angel was a scheming, murderous, killing machine bitch. She couldn't be trusted. They wanted Angel to die so that the two of them could move on.

Twelve

The Russian Mafia

Angel was sought after by the Russians. They had money and her pictures from Gabriel's father. The Russian mafia was unlike any other family; they came for your blood when they came after you. Gabriel hoped to hear about Angel's death soon. She wanted Angel to suffer because she would become a single parent, and she didn't know how to raise her daughter independently.

The Russians gathered outside Angel's club and apartment complexes and were also monitoring St. Louis's home. However, St. Louis suspected something was wrong. A black Tahoe would appear on different days parked down the street. He informed Angel that they were being watched by some influential people and that he would call in for some favors. He knew well that the Russians don't play, but he didn't want Angel to be too concerned because they had just discovered she was possibly pregnant.

St. Louis contacted a couple of people he knew to help him figure out who these men were. When St. Louis received a call back stating that Gabriel's father had placed the Russians to hit on Angel's life, he knew he needed to devise a plan to get Angel out of town for a while. But he also knew it wouldn't be easy to get past the Russians.

St. Louis knew he had to come up with a plan quickly because the Russians had three trucks watching each spot. When St. Louis told Angel that he wanted her to travel alone, Angel realized he attempted to save her from the Russians. So Angel devised her own strategy: if they wanted to her, they had to bring it. *With your soldiers and mine, we could bring Iraqi to Chicago, and those Russians wouldn't know what hit them*, Angel told St. Louis.

Angel and St. Louis gathered their troops for a meeting. They were going to take this killing to a whole new level, wildly, since the Russians had penetrated their territory. But, first, Angel had to return to the gun shop, where she knew a guy named Dakota. Angel knew Dakota felt bad for her, and she knew she could get him to do anything for her, so she had to use him to her advantage.

Angel didn't want to waste any time, so she called Dakota to see if he was at work. Dakota responded he was at work, and he invited her to come by and see him. Angel accepted Dakota's invitation, and thirty minutes later, Angel was walking through the door.

Angel had parked his truck behind the gun store. She told Dakota she had $50,000 for artillery and needed everything from missiles to hand grenades. She didn't want those Russians to come on anyone's turf again without thinking because they had to bring ass to get ass, and Angel was going to take as much ass as they brought.

The Russians planned to attack Angel in her apartment that night and blow up all her properties to force her to come out into the open. They didn't realize that Angel and St. Louis had an army of soldiers ready for war and were camped down the street from where the Russians had parked their Tahoe. Eastside, one of Angel's soldiers, was prepared with a missile in a van parked directly behind the Russians Tahoe. They would not make it back to their cars. They were going to die in the same way that Denzel Washington did on Training Day, but their fate would be far worse.

The Russians stepped out of their vehicles, armed with machine guns. They did not know that Angel's and St. Louis' army of soldiers would attack from every corner of Angel's entire block. So they lit them up like a Christmas tree. Angel's block was so loud that they couldn't hear the police sirens coming from afar. When Angel's soldiers realized the cops were on the set, they turned around and began blowing up the cop cars with hand grenades. The Russians sent to kill Angel couldn't even return home in body bags; the artillery Angel got from Dakota ripped through them like chopped beef in a supermarket.

Angel and St. Louis had enough soldiers to kill people from at least four states. They did, however, lose twenty people that night, but they could be replaced. It was a nightmare. When the other officers came, the media were everywhere. What they saw that night made them fear living in Chicago. People knew Chicago was much like any other town for the drug trade, but the deaths shocked the city. They wanted Angel and all other drug traffickers, like St. Louis, out of town.

Mr. Dane saw the news. He was shocked to learn that Angel had the power to kill the Russians he had sent to kill her. Mr. Dane thought that Mr. Salvador might have taught Angel survival skills because she could hear a mouse crawl across a cotton floor. He knew he had to sort the mess out because he was the reason for the Russians' death after sending them to kill Angel. Mr. Dane also knew his family was in danger because the Russian mafia had them on a hit list, so he had to get his family somewhere safe.

Since the street killing spree, Mr. Dane didn't know that St. Louis had paid off the Russian mafia family to keep him and Angel alone. He also told Russians that coming at them from the side would be risky because their force matched theirs. He was the mafia kingpin of Chicago, and no one would chase him away from his city.

Mr. Dane had his family moved two days later. He dispatched ten of his best bodyguards to transport his family to one of his safe houses in Montana, where they would be safe. He told his wife that he would be close behind them once his family had left in a couple of days. Mr. Dane attempted to arrange a meeting with Boris, the head of the Russian mafia. Boris agreed to the meeting because two of the Russians killed by Angel and her soldiers were Boris's sons.

Mr. Boris demanded someone's head in retaliation for the deaths of his two sons. He was curious what favor his sons owed Mr. Dane. He should have talked to him before sending his sons on a mission to kill someone. Mr. Dane met Mr. Boris at a restaurant with his wife, Isabella. Mr. Boris wanted Mr. Dane to see her tears of grief at her son's death. Instead, Mr. Dane gazed at Isabella, hurt. He knew Angel was a trained killer, but he didn't realize Angel was that deranged.

Mr. Dane spoke with Mr. Boris and expressed his condolences for his loss. He also told Mr. Boris that his two sons owed him a favor because one night, when they were out drinking, they raped a sixteen-year-old young lady who was walking home from a party. They didn't want him to know what they had done, so they went to Mr. Dane to clean up their mess.

Mr. Boris appreciated his help, but now his sons were dead because some half-breed bitch took their lives. He wanted to know where Angel lived because she wanted her to feel like suffering losing a child.

You have two children yourself, don't you? Mr. Boris asked Mr. Dane.

Yes, Mr. Dane replied.

He didn't know why he had asked him that question, but what Mr. Boris said next caused Mr. Dane to reach over the table and punch Mr. Boris in the mouth.

I've killed your bodyguards and will keep your wife and daughters safe until you kill Angel. After the job is completed, you will reunite with your family. If you don't bring me Angel Carter's head, your wife and daughters' heads will be delivered to you in a hatbox. Do you understand? Mr. Boris said.

Mr. Dane was so enraged that he agreed to go kill Angel himself. Because his daughter and Angel grew up together, he believed he could get close to her.

Mr. Dane had set out on a suicide mission. He was going to murder Angel because he wanted nothing wrong to happen to his family. Mr. Dane traveled to Chicago with ten of his personal bodyguards. He knew Angel had her own private army, so he devised a strategy to persuade her to meet him alone. St. Louis wouldn't even let Angel go to the restroom alone, so attempting to get Angel alone would never happen.

Mr. Dane arrived in Chicago three days later. Later that day, he called Angel to let her know he was in town and wanted to see her. She agreed to meet with him, but only in a secluded area on her property. Of course, he wasn't expecting Angel to be so harsh with him. Still, Angel wasn't taking any chances with her life anymore. She had to be extra cautious, and St. Louis wouldn't let Angel go anywhere without him.

Mr. Dane arrived on time but was disappointed to find Angel's guards at the door, searching him and his two bodyguards. But Angel knew he was there for a reason. She was going to find out because these crime families were suddenly coming after her, and she knew Mr. Dane was coming next, so she wanted to hear what he had to say. Angel knew that if he mentioned her fake ass mafia crime family, the Salvador's, she'd split his wig wide open.

Mr. Dane started by asking Angel how she was doing.

"I've been all right. Now I know you didn't travel all the way to Chicago to check on me. Why didn't you come to see how I was when my family was murdered?" Angel said.

When that went down with Angel's family, he lied and said he was out of town on business. He also expressed his condolences for Angel's loss and stated that he was now present.

Angel had the impression that Mr. Dane was thinking about something, but she kept her thoughts to herself. She wanted him to speak or forever remain silent because she had the final say when all was said and done.

To clear the air, Mr. Dane asked Angel if she had seen Gabriel. He informed her that her mother had spoken with her and discovered that they would-be grandparents. What he had just said to Angel caused the hair on the back of her neck to stand up. *Oh, Gabriel is pregnant by Mike. That hoe won't have that baby if I have anything to do with it.* Angel thought to herself.

Angel became disgusted looking at Mr. Dane. She was curious why he was there. Angel felt uneasy, so she decided to dump the shit on the table.

"I know you set up the Russian guys to come here and kill me, Mr. Dane."

Mr. Dane's eyeglasses fell from his eyes to his nose when she said that. He took a step back to get a better look at Angel to see if she was joking.

Angel snapped her fingers, and St. Louis emerged from the back with an alligator. He had it trained to eat in the blink of an eye. Then, to show that he had the alligator trained on point, St. Louis told the alligator to stand over by Mr. Dane.

"Mr. Dane, Mr. Dane, Mr. Dane, Mr. Dane, Mr. Dane, Mr. Dane, Mr. Dane, Mr. Dane, I'll ask you once why you're here, and if you lie to me or my woman, my alligator Ralph will eat your bodyguards one by one." St. Louis said.

Mr. Dane stared at St. Louis as if he were insane. *I don't care about my bodyguards. They are compensated for their efforts on my behalf. Their job is to protect me by any means necessary.* He said.

Before Mr. Dane could finish his sentence, his bodyguard Tommy began speaking as if he had verbal diarrhea. He didn't want to become the alligator's food, so he looked at Angel, almost pleading for his life. He knew that if they got out of there alive, he'd die at Mr. Dane's hands.

Angel had seen enough. She wanted the alligator to have his dinner. So she told St. Louis to fuck the small talk and get down to business because she had a doctor's appointment she didn't want to miss. After the alligator had dinner—the two bodyguards, Mr. Dane was next, and he wasn't afraid to die.

Even if you kill me, you won't be safe because more crime families like mine want you dead, bitch, so you better watch your back because they won't stop until they put your ass in the dirt, he told Angel.

Angel confronted Mr. Dane, spit in his face, and declared. *I'm going to kill your entire family, especially your pregnant ass daughter, so you can go straight to hell. Maybe I'll see you there one day.*

Thirteen

～

Amy Leaving Chicago

Amy knew she had to leave town when she discovered it was Angel who took her son Conner, but she was in love with Angel's older brother David. She hated leaving David, but he didn't want to abandon his brother and sister. Still, when David and Dante realized Angel was a loose cannon, they needed to distance themselves from her. Little did they know, Angel had planned to put them to sleep for good.

Angel was on her way to her club when she saw a girl who looked like Amy, which piqued Angel's interest. Now that David is dead, she can continue to take Amy's son Conner. Angel hated Amy because they would not have learned about her illegal baby-selling business if she hadn't dated her brother. Angel went to Amy's place after her club to see if she still lived there. When Angel arrived at Amy's apartment, she was disappointed. She had left. Angel didn't know where, but she'd find her.

Angel needed to know where Amy was, so she contacted Mr. Hayes once more and placed him on retainer to locate Amy and her son. Angel gave Mr. Hayes pictures of Amy and her son. She knew nothing about Amy to provide him with the information he needed to find her, but she didn't mind as long as he tried.

While Angel was looking for Amy at her apartment, Amy was on a redeye flight to Montana to see her mother. Amy knew Angel would look for her as soon as she crossed her mind again, so she needed to get her baby boy out of harm's way. Amy hadn't spoken to her mother in four years, and it was time to make a visit. She hoped everything to be alright when she returned and introduced her to her grandson.

Amy was afraid to knock on her mother's door when she arrived in Montana. Amy was surprised to see her mother standing with open arms when the door swung open. Her mother was thrilled to see her. For years, she assumed her daughter had died. She hired private investigators, but they could not locate her. Amy's appearance after four years without even a letter or postcard was precisely what she had hoped for: a chance to be reunited with her daughter. Amy's mother didn't realize she wasn't there for herself, but she was there to make sure Angel didn't find her son.

Amy told her mother where she had been and what she had been up to for four years. She also told her about Angel and the kidnapping of her son. Her mother was astounded. She couldn't believe her daughter had been through so much at such a young age. She mostly blamed herself because Amy would not have been molested by her stepfather if she had spent more time at home. But, unfortunately, she was so busy working that she forgot she had a little daughter who needed her guidance.

Amy told her mother she forgave her for her flaws and that she just wanted the two of them to move on. Her mother had waited four years to hear her daughter say it, and it warmed her heart. She had forgiveness from God, now she had it from her daughter, and she had peace.

Amy's mother wanted to know who Conner's father was because he could keep Conner safe and away from Angel. Amy informed her that Conner's father's name was Ronald Louis. They had sex once, and she never told him about Conner. He didn't even know he had a son.

Do you know how to contact him? Amy's mother inquired.

Yes, he lives in Chicago, where I am from. Because he's a drug lord, I didn't want him to know about our son. I wanted my son to have a normal life, not live in the shadow of his father's drug dealing. She responded.

"I understand what you're saying, Amy, but your son needed his father's help in protecting him from that crazy, deranged woman, Angel."

"Mother, rumor has it that Ronald is dating Angel. I'm not sure how true it is, but her brother David, whom I was dating, told me she was before Angel killed him."

"Angel murdered her own brother?"

"Yes, she did, and she intends to murder me, kidnap my son, and sell him to the highest bidder in her black market baby-selling business."

"Oh, Amy, you need to go to the police station."

I'm afraid I can't do it, Mother. She has so much money that she employs half of the police force and the judges. I don't want to take that risk until my son is safe. I don't even feel safe now because Montana is still not far enough. I wanted to go back to Chicago to set Angel up to get busted, but I didn't know who to trust in the police force. Amy explained.

Amy's mother was relieved to see her daughter return home, but what Amy told her terrified her. She was scared for her daughter and grandson, as well as for her own life. She knew she had to come up with something to help Amy. She knew a couple of people working underground to help women in danger of being abused by their husbands. She called them, and they gave her a phone number to call at a payphone they had set up for women to use. Amy called them, and she and Conner were rushed out of the house at 2:30 a.m. to a safe place.

Amy left her mother's house just in time because Mr. Hayes was hot on her trail. How he knew where to find Amy's mother was a shot in the dark, but he was good at his job. The reason Angel kept him on retainer. Mr. Hayes monitored Amy's mother's house for four days. He saw no sign of Amy and Conner, so he decided to tap Amy's mother's phone line to see if she would contact her by phone, but Amy didn't call her mom. When Amy agreed to go underground, she could call no one.

Angel wondered if Mr. Hayes had found Amy. He was meant to call her in two days, but he hadn't. So she called him to ask for news. Mr. Hayes didn't want to answer the phone because he didn't have any information about Amy yet. Still, he did so to let Angel know he was in Montana and had found Amy's mother, but Amy wasn't there. But he knew she'd show up, eventually.

Amy was unhappy being underground because she didn't know anyone. She met a woman named Robin in the program she was in. Amy thought Robin was cool, but she was afraid to trust anyone. Angel had long arms and money, and she didn't want her to reach out and touch her without her knowing. Amy developed a close friendship with Robin. They and their children shared a bedroom. They both had boys, so Conner and Eddie got along fine. Amy and Robin became close like sisters, so Amy decided to tell Robin about her past one night.

Robin wasn't surprised by Amy's stories because she hid from her husband of ten years, who tried to slit her throat while she slept to get out of their marriage without paying her a dime. He was suing Robin for custody of their son Eddie, whom he had been sexually abusing since he was two—now Eddie was six, and she didn't want him to have her son.

Amy expressed her desire to retaliate against Angel to Robin. Robin stated she could find someone in the prosecutor's office who could assist her in stopping Angel's behavior and that Angel needed to be stopped. Robin also told Amy that she had never met a woman so heartless in her life. She even told Amy that she didn't believe Angel had a soul and that Amy had made the right decision to take her son underground for safety. Amy needs to stay out of Angel's reach if she is that dangerous.

Angel had plans for Amy. Once Mr. Hayes returned with information on Amy, she wanted Amy to pay for escaping from the house when she labored with Conner. In addition, Angel felt like Amy owed her for bringing her off the street when she was pregnant. Angel also despised the idea that Amy was dating her brother, and Amy didn't back off as she ordered her to.

Amy decided to travel back to Chicago to put the ball in motion to expose Angel's wrongdoings. Amy asked Robin to keep her little boy safe while she was gone. She was tired of running and hiding from Angel. She wanted to enjoy life with her son without hiding away and monitoring her back.

Mr. Hayes called Angel and said Amy was a no-show and hadn't even called her mother, so his trip was wasted. He told Angel that the trip was on him because this was his first defeat, and he hoped Angel would still keep him on retainer, and she said she would.

Angel said to Mr. Hayes. *"This woman is like smoke. She vanished without a trace, which was unbelievable. But, it's fine because she'll show up somewhere one day, and Angel Carter will be waiting."*

Angel's devilish side came out while she was speaking with Mr. Hayes. She regarded kidnapping Amy's mother to bring Amy out of hiding. She asked Mr. Hayes for Amy's mother's address to send someone to pick her up and bring her to Chicago. Mr. Hayes was delighted to provide Angel with the address because he was eager to leave Montana and return to his office. He had two more cases that he was neglecting because of Angel.

Amy informed Robin of her plans, and Robin was glad to keep Conner for her. Amy left after breakfast the following day to return to Chicago. Amy went to the police station when she arrived in Chicago. Amy became terrified when she saw one of Angel's officers. When he didn't notice her, Amy went upstairs and asked the officer at the desk to speak with the prosecutor. Instead, Amy was instructed to sign her name on the sign-in sheet and take a seat. Amy was escorted back to the prosecutor's office after waiting for twenty minutes. She smiled, knowing she was about to turn the tables on Angel Salvador, a.k.a. Angel Carter.

Fourteen

~~~

Angel Getting Busted

Amy provided an entire rundown on Angel Carter's business. She told the prosecutor about Angel's brothers' murders and even tried to kidnap her son to sell him. Angel was also in charge of six buildings that involved drug production, gambling, and child trafficking. Angel set up a hospital-style room in her basement for pregnant teenagers who had nowhere to go. She would murder them right after they gave birth so she could sell their babies on the black market.

Mr. John Jones, the prosecutor, had once worked for Angel's brothers. So Amy's testimony did not surprise him at all. He is up for reelection, and taking down someone of Angel Carter's caliber would be right up his alley.

Mr. Jones knew well that it involved Angel in almost everything Chicago offered. So he inferred that if he was going to defy her, he should put all his eggs in one basket. The prosecutor knew somebody was running Chicago, and to hear it was a woman, he needed to meet this Angel Carter in person.

He called a phone meeting with the commissioner to shut down Angel's businesses and arrest her. However, to get a judge to sign a warrant, he needed to have substantial evidence. So Mr. Jones spied on the people who frequently come to Angel's establishments. He needed to photograph people entering and exiting the buildings. Mr. Jones monitored Angel's place for two weeks. What he saw coming out of Angel's building next astounded him. It was Judge Clinton Blake, the judge he had taken his case about Angel Carter to.

He knew some shady things were going on and wanted to get a little closer to the situation, so he went to Angel's strip club to see if he could get a pass. One night, Mr. Jones saw one of Angel's strippers, Casey, leaving the club and propositioned her.

Did you want to make a thousand dollars? He asked.

What I got to do for you? Casey replied.

I just need you to get me into Club Sophistication, that's all. Mr. Jones remarked.

She responded, *"Mister, for a thousand dollars, I would get you a backstage pass to Halle Berry's dressing room. Give me my thousand dollars, and we can go in right now."*

Casey escorted Mr. Jones into the club, where he sat in a corner, taking photos of everyone there. The judge was getting a lap dance from one stripper, and he was pulling twenties from his pocket like he had a hole in it. Then, finally, he thought to himself; I will blow the top off the Windy City of Chicago. It was going to be judges, lawyers, and police officers going down. He'd never seen so many city officials on the wrong side of law.

John realized he'd have to convince the judges and commissioner because he didn't know who he could trust with the city under Angel's grasp. So he went to the mayor with photos and voice recordings of conversations he had with undercover police officers he saw at the club that night. The officers were so high on the blow they snorted that night that they didn't notice John wasn't part of the game plan. Bringing their asses to the ground was his only purpose.

The following day, Mr. Jones called Amy to see if she would testify against Angel after her arrest. It relieved Amy that Angel was finally going to jail. Mr. Jones wanted to place Amy in protected custody, but he didn't know how long she would be there. Amy needed to know because she didn't want to be away from her son too long, but she wanted to see Angel's face once they locked her up, plus she wanted to tell St. Louis about their son. It was all she wrote when Mr. Jones convinced the mayor to find a judge he could trust to issue a warrant for Angel and her business.

Angel awoke the following day feeling ill. She told St. Louis that something was wrong and didn't feel safe because something was about to happen. She told St. Louis that she needed to rearrange some things.

"I want Amy's mother to be moved to our warehouse in Kansas City for the time being. Something isn't adding up, baby."

As soon as Angel moved Amy's mother, she received a phone call informing her that Johnny Law had taken over all of her businesses. They looked everywhere for Angel, but she was nowhere to be found. Angel had been staying at St. Louis' house. No one knew they were together, so they needed information from one of the undercover officers in their custody.

Hammer was truly put into David's and Dante's fold as an informant. He had enough information to lock them up for the rest of their lives. He had to act as if he had murdered his own son. Hammer didn't like his son, but he would not kill him for two wannabe kingpins. He had a dummy made to look like his son. It was so real that the people on the show couldn't have done it better. So when Hammer presented the deal to Mr. Jones, the prosecutor accepted because he now had two witnesses for the city of Chicago v. Angel Carter.

Angel was so worried that the police were on her trail, so she had to flee the Chicago area for a while until she had her baby. She would be a mother for the first time, and she would know what it was like to have that motherly bond with your child. Angel eventually ends up in Memphis. She went into hiding for four months. She had a baby girl, whom she named Gloria, after her deceased mother. Angel Carter was arrested two months after giving birth to her daughter when someone in Memphis saw her picture on the Most Wanted television show.

Fifteen

⌘

Abby and Gabriel

Abby had returned to Hawaii the night Angel had threatened her about her secret relationship with Mike. Angel was a twisted person, and Abby knew what she was up to, including the murder of her own family. So she trembled when she learned Mike had also died, as she was pregnant with his child.

Abby told her mother she was pregnant by a guy she met at a bar for a one-night stand, which turned her mother beet red from frustration.

Abby tried calling Gabriel, but she never answered her phone. She left a message after message, but she never got a return call from her. Abby just prayed that Angel did not have her goon squad kill Gabriel. She did not know that Mr. Boris, another mafia kingpin, was holding Gabriel prisoner, not Angel.

Now he was about to let Gabriel and her mother go since the job's done. Mr. Dane's death made his retribution sweeter. His family is experiencing the same pain as he and his wife.

Mr. Boris kept his word. He had his bodyguards drop Gabriel and her mother off at a bus station and told them they didn't owe the Russian family anymore.

Gabriel saw at least fifteen missed calls on her phone when they got home. She looked at her contacts and discovered that the 10 of them were from Abby. She decided to call Abby after taking a shower. Images of Mike rubbing her pregnant stomach flashed through her mind while she was in the shower. She broke into tears, losing not only Mike but also her father to her archenemy, Angel.

Abby decided to call Gabriel one more time before she gave up calling her. She wanted to know if Gabriel was alive, and if so, did she know Mike was dead.

When Abby called Gabriel for the eleventh time, Gabriel answered:

"Hi Abby"

Abby was so happy she started screaming.

"Gabriel, I thought Angel killed you."

"A Russian mafia boss, Mr. Boris, had kidnapped my mother and me," Gabriel stated.

"Oh my god, Gabriel, what the hell is going on. Did Angel team up with the Russian mafia?"

Are you all right?

Did they hurt you or your mother?

The Russian mafia is more dangerous than any other crime family.

Abby was shooting question after question at Gabriel and was talking so fast, until Gabriel said,

"Abby, calm down. We're fine."

Abby and Gabriel were on the phone when they heard on the television show "Most Wanted" saying they had finally captured Angel Salvador, a.k.a. Angel Carter. Angel Carter was unknown to Abby and Gabriel. They were trying to figure out who this Angel Carter was. They both wanted to travel to Angel's trial in Chicago to find out why they called her Angel Carter.

Gabriel asked Abby if she wanted to fly to Chicago to see what they had on Angel and if she had been charged with Mike's murder, too. They agreed to meet at the airport the following morning on the first flight to Chicago. When they got to the airport, they were amazed at their stomachs' matching months.

Abby asked Gabriel, *"What are you having, a boy or a girl?"*

"I am having a girl," Gabriel said

"I am having a little girl too," Abby told Gabriel

They didn't have to ask about their children's father because they both knew it was Mike.

When the plane landed in Chicago, Abby and Gabriel reserved a hotel room near the airport in case they needed to leave quickly. They settled into their rooms and planned to meet for supper. After supper, they took a cab to Angel's arraignment to see whether she would make a bond.

Angel was charged with racketeering, murder, drug trafficking, black market baby-selling, and money laundering. Her bond was set at a million dollars, and St. Louis was on hand to bond her out, but they would not let her go so quickly. She was placed under house arrest and had to return home. St. Louis hired a badass attorney named Steven Blake. He was a black criminal attorney who the prosecutor despised because he won every case he took. Steven Blake was a well-known lawyer. He was also an expensive lawyer, charging three thousand dollars an hour. Angel paid every penny to ensure she didn't go to jail.

Angel looked tense throughout the court hearing that she didn't see Gabriel and Abby in the courtroom, staring at her with death in their eyes. Abby noticed a woman was sitting, holding a pretty little baby in her arms while the trial was ongoing, and Angel kept looking back at her. Abby and Gabriel did not know Angel just had a baby, so they followed the woman to the restroom to verify their suspicions.

"Oh, what a pretty little baby! Can I hold him?" Abby said to the woman.

"Her name is Gloria Carter, and she is a girl," the woman stated.

Abby and Gabriel were gasping for air, unable to believe Angel had given birth and Mike might also be the father.

Gabriel came up with an idea to kidnap Angel's baby to let her feel how it felt to lose someone you love. She told Abby what she was thinking but, Abby wasn't down with it because she knew Angel could still kill them even if she was on trial for all these other crimes. Besides, kidnapping her baby would be a murder sentence for real.

Gabriel thought Abby didn't want to take revenge as she feared Angel would put them through hell, but Gabriel wanted vengeance. She desired for Angel's heart to be as empty as hers. Gabriel didn't know Angel for real. For a long time, Angel's heart was empty, the reason she had been through the motions of all her wrongdoings.

That morning of her trial, Angel got out of jail. She was relieved to hold her Baby Girl for a while. But while Angel was at home with her daughter, the prosecuting team dug deeper into Angel's past, assuring her demise.

After being released from jail, Angel got up the following morning and began making plans for her child if Mr. Blake could not clear her of her charges. First, she wanted to make sure Gloria would be all right. Angel loved her daughter and promised she'd never had to go through what she had. She also talked to St. Louis about changing his career for their kid's sake, so if she ended up in jail, their daughter would have one parent to rely on.

"Stop talking like that because we have an attorney who eats sharks for lunch. You won't spend another day in jail. Wait and see," St. Louis said.

What St. Louis told Angel made her believe he was up to something. She knew he was a master at getting things done, especially for her. But she didn't realize St. Louis had a hit out on everyone involved in her trial, including the judge. He's going to make sure that no one went up against Angel.

Angel was in her room breastfeeding her baby while watching the news when a reporter revealed photos of the judge at her trial hanging naked from a bridge in downtown Chicago. Angel thought her man would only look out for her. However, St. Louis had already grabbed and held everyone investigating Angel until the jurors were finished. He was on his way to the prosecuting attorney's house when the judge was murdered. He had gone to their homes and burned them while they slept.

Angel was feeling bad deep inside. Angel missed her girlfriends, but she couldn't get over their betrayal of sleeping with her boyfriend Mike, who she later found was her brother by her father.

I should call Abby and Gabriel just to see if those two bitches will answer my call. Angel thought.

She did not know they wanted to talk to her too, especially Gabriel, who wanted to get close enough to Angel to cut her throat for killing her father and Mike. Still, Gabriel lacked the courage to do so.

Abby decided it was time to leave Chicago but wanted to return when Angel's trial resumed for the second time. She wanted her baby to be born before going back to the shy town. She was exhausted and swollen from carrying her baby. Abby had gained so much weight that she felt like the Goodyear blimp.

Abby's and Gabriel's due dates were three days apart, and they promised each other that they would let their daughters grow up together as sisters.

Gabriel wanted to make sure if Mike fathered Angel's daughter because she didn't want her to grow up alone. If Angel goes to jail, she figured she might get custody of her and raise her with her sisters. Abby and Gabriel talked about Angel's child and what she would have to go through if Angel were imprisoned, but it was heartbreaking what they saw on the news. Everyone on the legal side of the trial was dropping like flies; someone was killing them all.

Abby was talking to Gabriel on the phone on a Monday night. They were both confident it was time to bounce.

"*Do you think Angel had all those people killed? We both know that Angel's elevator does not go all the way to the top floor. So we really need to stop her. She needs to pay for everything, and if she doesn't go to jail time, she's going to burn in hell for what she's done for sure,*" Abby said.

"*There is some real gangster shit going on here. Angel might have hooked up with a guy just as deadly as she is. We, of all people, know that St. Louis is a man who could kill you in the blink of an eye. He'd been to jail several times and never spent a day. He knows people in high places and has killed everyone involved with his cases.*" Gabriel said.

While they were still on the phone, Abby's water broke. Soon after, she experienced labor pains.

"*Stay on the phone. I'm going to call an ambulance to pick you up. Just don't push it, okay?*" Said Gabriel.

While Gabriel was on the phone with the ambulance crew, her water also broke. So they sent an ambulance to pick her up, too.

Abby and Gabriel had two beautiful baby girls. They even weighed the same: eight pounds, seven ounces, and nineteen inches long.

Abby named her baby Sophia, and Gabriel named her daughter Michelle. They thought it was as close as they could get to Mike. Their daughters looked so much alike, like they were scanned. If Mike was alive, he couldn't deny either of their daughters because they looked just like their father.

Sixteen

∾

Isabella Stallone

Angel had become so engrossed in her trail that she had forgotten about her appointment with Helen Davis at the family services division. She told Helen she wanted to give some money to the families in the communal housing who needed help. That's how she got an early appointment. Angel was rushed back to Helen's office when she arrived at the division of family services. Helen stared like she saw a ghost when Angel entered her office because her daughter Isabella and Angel could be mistaken for twins.

Angel sat and looked at Helen before saying anything because she didn't want to come out and ask her about her father. Helen asked Angel who her parents were because she looked so familiar. Angel told Helen about her upbringing as the daughter of a kingpin. She even mentioned her mother to Helen. Helen was astounded by what she heard.

Helen knew Cane was married when she started dating him. They've been seeing for a short while. He told Angel he loved his wife, and he would not leave her. He just wanted to dibble around in the street for a time, but Helen fell head over heels in love with Cane. Helen told him her feelings, but Cane told her their little playtime was over. She was devastated and upset about how their relationship turned out, and she became very ill. Helen had to be admitted to the hospital for observation and found out that she was pregnant. Helen didn't want Cane to find out she was pregnant. She wanted him to stay away from her. It wasn't his fault that Helen developed feelings for him. Cane told her before they jumped into bed together that he had a family. He just needed someone other than his wife to satisfy his sexual appetite.

Hearing Helen says all those things about her father made her want to throw up, but she kept her cool down. Angel finally told Helen who her father was. She was so composed because she knew she was going to make Helen hate her later. Helen disrespected her mother by sleeping with her husband, but Angel needed to meet her sister. She wanted to get in touch with her. Angel saw a picture of Isabella sitting at Helen's desk and immediately got a headache because it was the same Isabella who was dating her brother, Dante. Angel thought, *"Chicago is too fucking small. She was right in my grill the whole time, and I didn't even notice her."*

Helen informed Angel that her daughter, Isabella, was a prosecuting attorney who worked downtown at the Seventh District. Angel felt as if she had been kicked in the stomach. How could both daughters be on opposing sides of the law? Angel called St. Louis to give information about her sister. *"Do you remember when I told you that my father had another daughter by a woman named Helen Davis?"*

"Yes. So what's up, baby? So tell me, what's going on? Are you all right?" He said.

Angel was on her way home when she felt like being followed. She looked at her rearview mirror and saw a black Crown Victoria tailing her. Angel called St. Louis and informed him of the situation. St. Louis told Angel that police detectives drive Crown Victoria and to keep going until she arrived home.

"Don't worry about it. You bring it home to me, and I'll handle it once you arrive. Hurry, baby, I'm going to have the garage door open and waiting for you to pull in." St. Louis said.

The Crown Victoria pulled over across the street as Angel got into the garage.

St. Louis snuck out of his back door with his Eagle machine gun and shot both men in the back of their heads.

He got into the car with the dead detectives and drove away. He drove about six miles down a dirt road, rolled their vehicle off a deep cliff, and the car exploded with fire and smoke at the bottom of the cliff. *"No one mess with my woman. You will die if you play with me without consequences."* He thought.

Angel worried when St. Louis didn't pick up the phone. She knew her man was smooth about everything he did. His name should have been clean. Angel had Isabella's phone number and wanted to call her for a lunch date at her house, but she didn't want to scare her off. Because, with all the press and camera crews hanging out around Angel Carter's house, Isabella might have known the person Angel Carter was. Isabella was on the other side of the law, so she would have to be blindfolded even to enter Angel's house.

After Angel left her office, Helen called Isabella. She didn't want Angel simply walking up to her daughter. Helen knew well that Angel was a stone killer. She didn't want her daughter to befriend Angel, but she wanted them to meet once. Helen thought Angel would be imprisoned once her trial was stalled, anyway. So she didn't have to be concerned about Angel destroying her daughter's reputation. Isabella knew more about Angel. She knew she was a kingpin's daughter with killer instincts, like a man on death row. Isabella also knew Angel was associated with St. Louis, a Chicago-area drug lord. So she was bad news all around.

Helen had told Isabella her father was a mechanic named Harold Stallone, who worked on Broadway Street.

Helen recalled what her mother had always told her as a child. *"The things you do in the dark will soon come to light."* She couldn't help but cry because what her mother had said was so true. Her sin of sleeping with a Hawaiian kingpin had come back to bite her in the ass. Helen made Angel promise not to tell her daughter about their father until she told her. She didn't want Isabella to find out the things she should have told her years ago. Harold wanted to be Isabella's father because Isabella was only two weeks old when he met Helen. Cane turned over his parental rights to Harold when Helen told him she was pregnant. Cane never spoke of Isabella nor acknowledged she was his daughter.

Angel kept her promise. She met Isabella on her terms. Isabella wanted Angel to meet her at an art museum, where there would be lots of people hanging out. Isabella stumbled why Angel wants to meet her, of all people. She wondered what she wanted to talk to her about because she wasn't the prosecutor on her case. *"So what on God's green earth did she have to talk with her about?"* She thought.

Isabella called her mother to let her know she was going to a museum to meet with Angel Carter. She warned Isabella to be cautious and keep a close eye on her because Angel had everyone in the Tri-state area looking for her.

I know, Mother. I will not waste my time talking to a well-known serial killer like Angel Carter. She is wanted for all kinds of things. What is so messed up is that her case came across my desk today. Isabella said.

Before Isabella could say another word, her mother told her. *"Let someone else handle that case because everyone that has enough nerves to stand up against Angel was now dead." So please, Isabella, let them white folks fight their own battles this time. Do not let them get you killed by going up against Angel Carter. She plays for keeps. She has more soldiers than men on the entire police force."*

Isabella pondered what her mother had just said. She knew her mother was right. Everyone on the force was terrified of going after Angel Carter. They knew Angel had the power to make even the mayor of Chicago bow down to her, and if he didn't, she'd wipe out his entire family. Isabella suspected Angel wanted something vital from her. Still, she reasoned, Angel might have known her case arrived on her desk. Isabella also knew Angel had a slew of officials on her payroll. Still, she kept all information she had about Angel's case to herself.

Angel played it off to Isabella about her relationship with Dante. She knew Isabella from dating her brother, but they started nothing because Angel killed Dante three days after he and Isabella hooked up.

I just wanted to meet with you because I haven't seen you since my brother's death. I told Dante you were lovely, and he told me he liked you a lot. Angel said.

Isabella had a feeling Angel was up to something. She felt like telling her something, but she didn't. She did not want to be in Angel's company for much longer. Isabella kept on thinking about what her mother said to her. *"Be careful and watch your back."* It played back and forth in her head like a recorder.

Isabella recalled the words her grandmother used to say to her all the time. "If you sleep with dogs, you wake up with fleas." She was perplexed why she kept hearing it while speaking with Angel. Her feminine instincts kicked in, so she cut off the meeting. She instructed Angel to contact her office to schedule an appointment the next time she needed to speak with her.

Angel looked at Isabella and said, *"Bitch, do you know who I am?"*

"Of course I do, bitch. You are a criminal who's wanted across the fucking map. So like I said, if you want to meet me again, call my office for an appointment." Isabella responded.

Angel raged. Isabella made Angel back down, which is unusual for her. Angel understood that she and Isabella were Cane's daughters and that if she got Isabella on her side, they might do some harm. Isabella was about to find out what Angel was after.

Seventeen

༄

Flipping the Scrip

Angel's court day was fast approaching, and it was only two months until her trial began. Angel felt confident that her man had taken care of everything. But, on the other hand, everyone handling her case had been killed, so she assumed it would be a long time before they found someone to prosecute her case.

Angel received a handwritten letter from the prosecutor's office two weeks before her trial. A new prosecutor had been assigned, and it was her half-sister, Isabella Stallone. Angel smiled to herself because, in her mind, she had the upper hand in shutting down Isabella. All she had to do was tell her attorney that she and Isabella were sisters. There would be a conflict of interest, and it would throw Isabella off her case. Angel did not know her case would be front-page news for years to come.

Angel waited for all the madness to end, so she became prepared when her court trial date arrived. She told St. Louis that once the case was over, they could marry and raise their daughter. But, unfortunately, Angel didn't realize that St. Louis had enough information to send her to the gas chamber.

Angel's trial began, and everyone, including Amy, Gabriel, and Abby, was present. They were all in the first row, waiting to see Angel get fried.

Isabella called Aaron Morgan, a.k.a. Hammer, to testify against Angel in the first testimony of the day. First, he confessed to the court about what he did for the Salvador's. Next, Hammer testified in court that he was Dante and David's right-hand man.

Isabella started questioning Hammer. *"What do you mean right-hand man?"*

Hammer paused and looked at Isabella. *"Well, I'm a hired assassin."*

"Mr. Morgan, could you tell the court what you did for the Salvador's and how much they paid you as a hired assassin?"

"The Salvador family paid me $3,000 per week and another $2,000 to be their chauffeur."

"Mr. Morgan, are you telling the court that the Salvador's paid you $5,000 per week?"

"Yes, and Angel Salvador paid me to dispose of three bodies on June 3. They were the Russians she killed in the street war."

"Alright, I respectfully submit my case, Your Honor," Isabella said.

"Mr. Blake, would you like to cross-examine Mr. Morgan?" The judge asked Angel's attorney.

"No, your Honor, but I would like to call Amy Anderson to the stand, Your Honor." Mr. Blake responded.

Amy was surprised that they knew she was there. She saw Mr. Hayes and the mayor, whom she spoke with about Angel. The mayor also had information that could put Angel away. St. Louis had paid everyone off to get Angel out of the way.

Both attorneys finished their closing arguments, and the jurors called for a recess. When the jurors went back into the courtroom with the verdict, everyone was nervous. If Angel were found guilty, she would be locked up for the rest of her life. St. Louis sat behind Angel at the defense table, assuring her everything would be fine. Angel didn't know St. Louis had given the prosecutor nails to her coffin.

The entire room fell silent as the foreman read the verdict. Angel was terrified for the first time in her life. Finally, Angel and her attorney stood up as the foreman read the verdict. Angel was found guilty through all the charges filed against her. The entire courtroom erupted, especially Amy, Gabriel, and Abby. They knew well Angel deserved it.

Angel was devastated. They had her dead right on everything she did, and all evidence against her was never thrown away. St. Louis was the only person she allowed to get close to her and had enough information to bury her. When she looked at St. Louis behind her, he told her with a grin on his face.

"I was the one who gave them everything they needed to bury your ass with." St. Louis said with his gaze fixed on Angel.

Cane, our father, was a low-down dim-motherfucker, and your attorney, Steven Hayes, says hello to your big brother. He's a Carter, too. St. Louis added.

Angel was shocked. The person she trusted the most was the one who sent her up the river for life.

Isabella and St. Louis had been dating for years. St. Louis adored Isabella, and they planned everything for Angel. St. Louis met Isabella on his way to a court trial one day and had been together for five years. They both played newcomers and came to Chicago to take over. St. Louis needed to gain Angel's trust. Still, he had to use all his patience not to kill Angel after she tried to rob his fortress.

Isabella wanted to take Angel's case to make sure she never saw the light of day again. She even met Angel's attorney, Steven Blake, and St. Louis, paid Steven to lose a case for the first time. Steven Blake has money, but when St. Louis approached him with a two-million-dollar offer, he knew Angel would go up the river without a paddle.

St. Louis had photographed Angel murdering Mr. Salvador and wiped out the entire family. He had documented the whole street war killings of the Russian mafia, but St. Louis wasn't in any photographs. He'd given Isabella everything he had against Angel and wanted her gone, but it was out of his hands once they gave her the chair.

Isabella knew who her father was from the beginning. She also knew Dante, David, and Angel were her family, but she didn't tell her mother because she planned to reveal it to her the day before Angel's trial.

When St. Louis discovered Angel and Isabella were his sisters, he felt green inside. He had a child with his sister, but he had some bad news for both of them. St. Louis had to keep Isabella around to stay out of jail. He lost all love for her when he discovered Isabella was trying to play him. He did a background check on Isabella and found that the Russian mafia placed her in the prosecutor's office. She was preparing him to be killed as soon as they apprehended Angel. Shortly after Angel's trial, St. Louis' plan is to have his brother, Steven Blake, assassinate Isabella.

Angel found herself speechless after that. She became numb as her entire life spiraled out of control. Steven followed Angel in the back, where they booted and suited her to be transferred to the women's prison. She was dumbfounded because they sentenced her to life in prison with no chance of parole, but she thought to herself, *"that punk had me fooled the entire time. We had a baby together, but it's fine because the payback is a bitch."*

Isabella thought that since Angel was out of the way, she could take her place with St. Louis until she got the code to his secret passage. However, because Angel attempted to rob him, St. Louis rearranged the entire room. St. Louis had a dummy safe installed in place of the old one. He also placed two rockwilders in the alarm system's area so they would greet anyone who entered with a rude awakening.

Isabella ran into Steven Blake on her way out of the courthouse. Steven invited her for a celebratory drink because she had won the case. Of course, she was thrilled to have won the case of the year.

Why not? Let's head over to Club Sexy. Isabella answered.

Before Steven could even respond, Isabella asked. "Would you like me to drive you there?"

"Since I asked you, I will appreciate it if you ride with me, and I will drop you off at your car," Steven calmly looked at her.

Isabella felt excited. *"Sounds like a plan. Let's go."*

As soon as they arrived at Club Sexy, Steven informed Isabella that he needed to use the restroom. Then, he crept out the back door of Club Sexy, jumped in his car, and drove ten blocks to cut the brake line to Isabella's car. When he returned to Club Sexy, Isabella was standing at a table, talking to one of her associates about Angel Carter's case.

Isabella noticed Steven as he exited the restroom and returned to their table. What she didn't see was Steven slipping a Mickey into her drink. She'd ordered a Hennessey and Coke for Steven and an apple martini for herself. They had two more drinks before they left. Isabella felt a little dizzy, so Steven asked if she was okay. Isabella assured Steven she would make it home and would call him once she arrived. Steven walked Isabella to her car and stood there watching her drove away. She was lightheaded from the Mickey Steven had put in her drink, and she could only see one side of the road.

Steven didn't hear from Isabella that night. So when he got up the following day to shower for work, he turned the television on to listen to the news. A woman had hit the side of the bridge, and her car exploded, killing her instantly. But because the news reporter didn't mention the woman's name, he wasn't sure if it was Isabella.

When Steven arrived at work that morning, everyone was standing around as if their best friend had died when he walked in.

Then one attorney threw out a question. "Did you see the news this morning?"

No, why? Steven replied.

"Isabella is dead. Her car hit the bridge last night and exploded." The attorney felt hesitant to complete the statement.

"You've got to be kidding, right? Isabella and I had drinks last night, and I dropped her off here to her car, and she appears to be fine." Steven said.

Isabella's mother, Helen, was so distraught. She knew her daughter would be next. Helen warned Isabella not to take Angel's case several times, but she still did, and now her daughter is dead. She wanted to visit Angel in jail and kill her with her bare hands. Helen didn't know Angel had anything to do with Isabella's death.

Steven went to his brother St. Louis' house to pick up his money for killing Isabella, but someone had already been there and ripped his house to shreds when he arrived. Steven stepped out the door. He did not know who had destroyed his brother's home, and he didn't want to be caught in a trap. Steven returned to his car. He pulled out his phone and phoned

St. Louis. On the second ring, St. Louis answered, but the voice on the other end was strange to him. It sounded like a Russian speaking to him in a language he had never heard. *"We have your brother, and he's going to die,"* the man said. Don't even think about paying a ransom because his life isn't worth it. Steven was so distraught. He realized he was dealing with some heavy hitters, and he wanted nothing to do with it.

A month passed. Angel heard Isabella was dead, and she wanted to see Steven so she could ask him to check on her daughter. She wanted him to know she set him up and hung him out to dry. Angel told Steven that she had billions of dollars in an offshore account and wouldn't kill him if he helped her buy out her time. Steven looked at Angel as if she knew something that he hadn't.

"I know you went to St. Louis, and he wasn't there, huh? Well, he'll never cross a rich bitch like me again, and I'll tell you something else, brother dear. If you don't turn over my conviction tonight, it will be your last when you close your eyes." Angel told Steven.

The words spat out like knives. Steven knew he was in trouble.

Angel was no longer worried about her daughter. She paid a nanny her entire life to look after her daughter if she would be imprisoned. Angel arranged it the day she went to court. Her daughter and nanny had already left for Ohio, where her nanny was born. Angel thoroughly investigated her daughter's nanny. She would not hand over her child to a psycho. She had to pretend to be concerned about her daughter to catch Steven off guard.

One Sunday night, St. Louis was found dead with half of his head blown off in a booth at Club Sexy. When the club closed that Saturday night, the Russian placed him there. They never found the murderer, and the police department never even attempted to solve his case. They looked at it as if another drug dealer bites the dust.

Eighteen

~∽~

In Bed with The Enemy

Steven paid another visit to Angel in jail. However, he had a different agenda this time. His mother told him that Cane Carter was his father. Still, his mother was an alcoholic who had been to several institutions for her drinking problems. She couldn't even recall having a child, so Steven was sent to his grandmother. Steven was raised by his grandmother from the age of two until he graduated from high school. When Steven returned home from signing up for college, he found his grandmother dead in the middle of the living room floor. She had died of a heart attack.

Following his grandmother's death, Steven went on to law school to become a badass lawyer. He graduated from law school with honors, opened his own law firm, and was well known in the Chicago area.

Steven looked into the whereabouts of his biological father. His father, in fact, was the Commissioner of the Chicago Police Department. He'd been in the same circle as his father for years. Steven was relieved because he didn't want to be a kingpin's son. However, he didn't want to be a commissioner's son, either. For him, how could a man of the Commissioner's caliber have sex with an alcoholic woman he arrested for prostitution in the back of his squad car, drop her off in an alley, and abandon her like trash.

Steven wanted to sit down with his father and pick his brain a little to see what kind of man he was. He wasn't ready to tell him he was his father yet. Steven intended to drop the bombshell on him as soon as his proof arrived at his office. He had a hair sample tested he got from the Commissioner's comb two days ago while the Commissioner was out for lunch. Steven infiltrated the Commissioner's office and stole his comb. He wanted to be certain that the Commissioner was his father before accusing him of being his deadbeat dad.

Steven didn't want the Commissioner to take on the responsibility of being his father. He wanted him to pay for what he had done to his mother. When the test results came in, he was a little nervous because he would have to pay for abusing his mother if he was really the Commissioner's son. Steven considers his mother to have been raped by someone supposed to serve and protect the law, not abuse it.

When Steven opened the envelope, he was surprised to see that their blood match was 99.99 percent. It turns out that his grandmother was correct about the Commissioner abusing his mother. Steven's mother also told his grandmother that he had sexual relations with Cane, the Hawaiian kingpin, before he was killed.

Steven had all the evidence he needed to confront the Commissioner. Still, he may need the information to buy himself some time in the future. Steven reflected on what Angel had said to him, so he returned to the jail to pay her another visit. Deep down, he cared deeply about Angel. He had liked her since the first day he took her on as a client, but he was never the type of guy to mix business and pleasure. He poured his heart out to Angel this time when he went to see her. Steven expressed his true feelings for Angel. He even told Angel that he wasn't her brother and that he had proof of it.

Why would I trust you? It was you and my barracuda sister who landed me here for the rest of my life. Angel asked while looking at Steven.

"I'm going to get your case overturned, and if I do, would you at least consider going out to dinner with me?" Steven said to Angel.

If you get my case overturned, I will go to dinner with you. But I can't promise I'll forget that you helped put me behind bars. Angel said.

I'm going to get started on your release right now. Steven said to Angel.

I need to go turn some stones and grease some palms before this case is over. I'll be back in a couple of days to see you. He added.

Steven was on a mission, and it wasn't for God, but he was going to need God's help.

Steven first went to the Commissioner's office and laid down the law. Then, he represented Angel the way he should have the first time. He told the Commissioner that he had evidence to bring the entire police department, some judges, the mayor, and the councilmen to their knees.

"You, sir, have a dirty trail behind you as well, commissioner." Steven explicated.

"You may have a law degree and street-smart, but you have no right to come into my office and threaten me," the Commissioner said to Steven.

Steven, tired of arguing with the Commissioner, instead said. *"Look, I don't really have a conflict with you yet, so here's some information that I think you should look at. If something happened to me, I want you to know that I have tapes and video recorders addressed to the Supreme Court waiting to be mailed. There would be a paper trail that would lead to everyone involved in these shambles. Since we're here, I'd like to ask you a question: Do you recall picking up a woman in your squad car for prostitution when you were a rookie cop about 36 years ago?"*

"Let me clear something up for you, young man. I can't even remember what I ate for dinner yesterday, let alone a woman I met 36 years ago."

Steven was becoming irate.

"Mr. Robert Harris, I know for a fact that you picked up a woman when you were a rookie cop. Tammy Blake was her name. She's my mother. You raped her, and I have proof because I am the result of that rape case," he claimed.

Mr. Harris looked at Steven as if he'd sprouted two heads. He inquired of Steven. *"Are you insane?"*

"I'm going to show you how crazy I am. If you don't help me overturn Angel Carter's case, you'll be sorry you ever met me." Steven stated.

Mr. Harris turned to face Steven and said. *"I'm not sure if I can assist you. Angel's case was a high-profile case, and bringing it up again will be a nightmare for everyone involved."*

"Everyone involved, including you, will be blown away if you don't help me. Is your wife aware that you raped a helpless woman when you were a shield and that you have a bastard son from a rape case you committed?" Steven added.

When Steven left the Commissioner's office that day, the Commissioner called and asked for some favors to overturn Angel's case. He could tell he was serious when he looked at his son. However, the Commissioner also glimpsed Steven. He knew he was his father even before Steven told him the results of the paternity test.

Mr. Harris needed to involve the judges in the videotapes that Steven had left him a copy of. Mr. Harris summoned the judges and requested a meeting in their chambers. When he arrived in the judge's chambers, both judges said to him, *"This better be important, Harris, because we have work to do and trials to hear."*

"Can you put this tape in my hand on your recorder?" Harris asked Judge Baker.

"Go ahead, but this better be good, Harris," Judge Baker said.

Judge Baker turned white as a sheet when he saw what was on the screen because he did not know Salvador's brothers were filming his sexual exploits. He had been outdone. He couldn't help but shake his head in defeat. But he knew he had to act quickly, or his wife would divorce him, and the media would eat him for lunch.

"But that's not all. There's one for you too, Judge O'Malley. You are right here." According to the Commissioner, while pointing at the video.

Judge O'Malley was the one getting screwed by a dog. It was disgusting to look at, but they needed to see who had their balls clamped in a pair of vise grips. They were all stunned and looked at each other.

"Harris, who did you get that tape from, and what do they want in return?" Judge Baker said, breaking the silence.

"Well, Your Honor, I received the tapes from Steven Blake. He stated he has more copies ready to be mailed to the Supreme Court if we do not assist him in having Angel Carter's case overturned."

"Is Steven Blake insane? Don't you realize we'll be disbarred if that case is even looked into?" Judge Baker stated.

"When Mr. Blake first came into my office with this information, I didn't think he had anything worth looking at until he showed me the tapes. But, unfortunately, he has everyone by the balls, so either we play ball with him, or we face jail time or worse."

"All right, we'll meet tonight at my house and see if we can find some light at the end of the tunnel because we're all having serious problems here." Judge O'Malley said.

That night, the three men agreed to meet. When the Commissioner left Judge Baker's chambers, he was furious. Judge Baker wanted to go after Steven, but he knew he couldn't because he had too much to lose, and he wasn't sure if Steven had letters ready to be mailed to the Supreme Court. Steven was in court on another case when he received a call from Judge Baker, who asked him to meet him in his chambers as soon as possible. Steven mused to himself. *"This had better not be a trap, but just in case, let me notify my people of what's about to happen."*

"You have guts to be messing around with the bigwigs." Judge Baker said to Steven.

"I hope you know what you're doing, son, because you're playing with fire." He added.

Steven agreed with the judge. He didn't deny that what he was doing was risky, but he just hoped everything would work out in the end. Judge Baker reminded Steven that Rome wasn't built in a day and that trying to get a high-profile case overturned would take time.

Steven Blake inquired of Judge Baker. *"How much time are you talking about because time is of the essence?" My client has a life she wants to resume."*

"Mr. Blake, how do we know that if and when your client is released, those tapes will not be sent to the Supreme Court?"

"First, allow me to correct you, Your Honor. It is when my client will be released."

"All right, Mr. Blake. What happens to those tapes when your client is released is what concerns me."

"You have my word on it. That those tapes will not be made available to anyone unless you guys make up your minds to go after my client or me."

"I guess we should get the ball rolling on your client's release, but we have one stipulation, and that is for your client to leave the city of Chicago. She is no longer welcome here, so upon her release, she must sell everything she owns and leave, never to return." Judge Baker said after considering what Steven had said.

Steven went to see Angel, informed her she would get out soon, and advised her to be patient. Angel was thrilled that Steven could make it happen so quickly, but she hadn't realized it would be a year before the judges could get all the paperwork in order.

Steven never imagined himself in bed with the enemy. Still, he made a promise to himself that he hoped he would never have to cross paths with the bigwigs again. Steven knew he had to move his law firm once Angel was released. He had to start over because he couldn't have a healthy growing business with so many people after him.

The city of Chicago would never be the same. There are too many illegal officials running the city into the ground, and the people have no voice. Everyone was afraid to speak up to anyone who might put a stop to what was going on. There is no one they can rely on. The entire city had been tainted.

Nineteen

༄

Angel's Release

Angel Carter finally hits the streets a year later. When she heard her name called to pack and stack it, she did not know what it meant, until one guard screamed. "Angel Carter, let's roll, we'll release you."

She was overjoyed. Steven Blake was waiting for her when Angel arrived at the front desk to retrieve her belongings and she couldn't believe Steven had kept his promise that he will have dinner with her. She was as hungry as a hostage. She smiled as she looked at him. He thought she had the loveliest smile he'd ever seen. But Angel had other plans for Steven. He was the best man for the job, but she needed her back cracked.

Angel planned to leave Chicago in two weeks, but first, she needed to get her affairs in order. She contacted a friend she met two years ago. Angel called Ramon to ask if she could talk to him about selling her assets. She had six flats, two stores, and a club.

Ramon told Angel to come and see him because he already had her covered. Ramon was someone she kept on standby in emergencies, and she was confident that he would be there for her. He was a heavy hitter and a Columbian mafia assassin who had a strong affection for Angel, but he never forced the issue as he knew angel would need him one day.

Angel was preparing to leave for Columbia when she saw Ramon waiting for her at the airport.

"Damn, Ramon, you're still as good as homemade wine."

"You wanted me to come over. Didn't you say so?"

Ramon gave her a smile.

"I just did to see if you would to go to Columbia."

"Let's go have lunch and discuss things over."

"Chicago wants you out but there is an alternative than selling your assets."

They wanted the judges to think she sold everything and had left the city.

"It's fine. I was planning to leave for a while to plan my next move."

"It's not over until Angela Carter says it's over, and you know what I mean. They won't be able to get rid of me so easily." Angel had a vengeful smile.

With Ramon's help, she set up all her businesses under dummy names and had a new firm called Top of the Line Incorporated. Ramon thought the company name suited her personality. The two stayed in touch.

Angel is ready to leave the Windy City. Her first stop was Ohio to get her daughter as she hadn't seen her in a year, then to California for the meantime.

When she got to Ohio, she found her daughter and nanny at the park and followed them home. When the nanny pulled into her driveway, she didn't notice Angel standing outside as she was so focused on hitting the baby in the car's backseat. That scene made Angel angry.

She went up to her car, pulled the nanny out of her daughter's sight.

"Leave my daughter in the car, bitch."

Now that Angel was back, she had to confront her about her daughter's mistreatment. The terrified nanny had no clue that Angel was now free.

She raised her 44 special magnum pistol to the nanny's head.

"How long have you been beating my daughter? If you lie to me, I'm going to splatter your brains all over your stainless steel refrigerator."

Hoping that Angel wouldn't kill her if she tells the truth, the nanny admitted she would beat the baby twice a day for crying without reason and she would not tolerate such behavior.

Angel slapped her face with the back of her pistol before she could finish her sentence and said.

"You should have lied to me, now you would never be a nanny to anyone again bitch."

Angel moved her daughter into her car, buckled her up, and drove away. Out of anger, Angel sped away, not caring if the nanny's neighbors heard the gunshots. The next-door neighbor heard the gunshots and called the police. She also described Angel's vehicle, a dark blue Ford with Chicago plates.

Angel knew someone heard the shots. Her gut tells her she would have to damage someone before going to Ohio to pick up her Baby Girl, So Angel stole the car before leaving Chicago. But she never imagined it would be her daughter's nanny.

After a few miles, Angel dumped the car and stole another, and after leaving Ohio, she bought a Ford Explorer and drove to San Diego, California, where she camped for a while. She rented an apartment because she never intended to make California her home.

She was thinking, *"After I get settled, I would give Steven a call to see how he was doing."*

But, before she had two days to settle, Angel got a call from Steven saying he's gone to San Diego to start a new firm. Although Steven had assisted her in escaping, he was also the reason she's taken away, so she wasn't sure how she felt.

Steven asked Angel where she was, but she hesitated to tell him she was also in San Diego. But she told him anyway it wasn't like he couldn't find out, regardless.

Because they were in the same state, Steven saw an opportunity to become more than just Angel's friend and get closer to her daughter. Having no children, he thought that becoming a father to Angel's daughter would be a start. So he asked Angel if he could come by to see her and her daughter and bring dinner.

"Of course, you could come by; besides, I need some company. Maybe I can relax a little with some adult conversation." Angel answered.

"I'd be there at seven. Is Chinese food okay?" Steven is excited.

"I'm sure it would be for us, but I don't think it would be proper food for my daughter. She's only one." Angel said.

"All right, how about I stop at the grocery store and pick up some baby food?" Steven offered.

"No. But thanks anyway, Gloria has plenty of baby food here."

"All right, is there anything else you want me to bring?" Steven asked.

"Yes, you can bring a bottle of white wine."

"See you at seven then."

Angel was sitting, watching the news, when the doorbell rang. It was Steven, always on time. While Angel was directing Steven to the kitchen, she overheard a news reporter said that they had found a woman in Ohio who had been shot in the face with a forty-five pistol.

Angel stood looking with a half-smile on her face, saying to herself, *"That bitch will never hit another child, especially not mine."*

Steven and Angel had a nice dinner together. They retreated from the kitchen into the living room, where they finished a bottle of wine. Angel started feeling hot and bothered. She stared Steven the eye, letting him know it was okay to make a move if he wanted to. Before she could get the thought out of her mind, Steven was all over Angel and didn't even stop him from strapping up.

She thought to herself, *"What the hell? I will not get pregnant."*

They started seeing each other regularly and did a lot of things together with her daughter. She started feeling like a family, but she couldn't shake the feeling that he hung her out to the wolves. Angel knew there would be nothing serious with her and Steven because she would never trust him, and one day, she was going to kill him.

One evening, Steven and Angel were at the mall when she saw Abby pushing a baby stroller. Angel wanted to speak to Abby.

"What the hell? She has her baby with her, and I have mine, so there would not be any arguing around children. Plus, I need her to see my spouse to be attorney Steven Blake." Angel thought.

When Angel approached Abby, she was tense. She knew Angel was lethal, and if she wanted her head, killing her in the middle of the mall wouldn't bother Angel. So Abby tried to play it cool to see what Angel had to say to her.

It shocked Abby when Angel spoke to her and asked.

"What is your daughter's name?"

"My daughter's name is Sophia." Abby answered.

Abby knew not to take any chances with Angel because she was a known killer. She knew that going up against Angel was like guerrilla warfare. California was big, but she had to hurry. Abby jump in her car and drove back to her apartment and as soon as she arrived, she started packing.

On her way to the airport to catch a flight back to Hawaii, she called her mother and said that she saw Angel with her lawyer-boyfriend at the mall. Abby told her mom she did not know Angel was free from prison. She also told her mom that something odd was going on because the evidence on Angel should have landed her in jail for the rest of her life.

Fire fueled Angel when she ran up to Abby at the mall. She wanted to drop Abby where she stood. She recalled the day she was sentenced and saw Abby and Gabriel smiling. It seemed as if they were happy that she would spend the rest of her life in prison, but they didn't realize she was going to be released.

Angel lay awake that night crafting a plan to conclude her unfinished business in Chicago and tie up some loose ends. She also wanted to rock some people to sleep. While her mind was wandering, a light popped into her head. It was time to hire a surgeon to reconstruct her entire body with a makeover. She didn't want to waste another night getting back at the people who tried to seal her faith.

Angel went online after seeing an ad for a two-bedroom loft on the outskirts of Chicago that she wanted to buy. She's now back in charge and trusted no one. Angel bought the loft and secured it like a New York state prison, with a theft-proof computer system. She even had a bank security system installed in her bedroom closet, although most of her money was in offshore accounts.

Angel wanted her return to be bold, with a statement that she is *"Angel Carter"* and that no one should ever forget it.

Angel didn't want to hurt innocent people, but those she was hunting would burn in hell for everyday she spent in prison. Ready to start a fire in Chicago, she bought a white Cadillac and Mercedes and had cards made up with her picture on them. She wanted them to think she was an investor and a real estate broker.

Her first move was to get her mother's club back to the family. So she would go to Club Sexy every weekend and talk to the owner to sell the club to her for a hundred thousand dollars in cash. She met up with the owner of Club Sexy that morning at a hotel. He came with the deed to the club, and Angel showed him the hundred thousand dollars. When the club owner reached down to grab the suitcase, Angel came from behind him and cut his throat from ear to ear. He bled to death on the hotel room floor.

Angel had no remorse because he took over her mother's club, stole the deed from her safe and had the guts to white-out her name and replace it with his. So why would she show any for him?

Angel was on high alert, like a shark in a feeding frenzy. She was full of anger that she wanted to crack down her enemies one by one. Next is the lawyer, Mr. Hayes, who shared her information with her sister Isabella, and for that, he was going to die in public for everyone to see.

She set up an appointment with Mr. Hayes as a new client and pretended to ask him to locate her long-lost brother. He looked at Angel like she's some fallen angel, couldn't stop his leg from shaking like a nervous wreck.

Angel provided him with fake information that led him to a vacant house where she waited for him. However, when he arrived at the location, it didn't look empty, so Mr. Hayes went inside and saw Angel standing dressed in all red.

"Look at me real good because I'm going to be the last you'll see in your life."

Mr. Hayes was afraid because he remembered her voice now, but he didn't recognize her voice in his office earlier. Mr. Hayes almost passed out as Angel came out into the light because he thought Angel Carter was on Rikers Island.

Angel said, *"When you were in court, you said loud, clear and confident that I was a stone killer, but you know what? That part was very true because what I'm about to do to you now will reveal who you truly are."*

Angel wore her twin Rutgers machine guns around her waist. She told Mr. Hayes to remove his clothes and toss them to her. Mr. Hayes did what Angel told him to do because he knew he should never play with her. He took off his clothes and threw them at Angel.

Angel told Mr. Hayes to get down on all fours. She'd broken off a broomstick and stuck the handle up Mr. Hayes's ass to show him what it was like to be fucked. After Mr. Hayes screamed, Angel used a switchblade to remove his penis, then took his body and shot holes all over it. Then, after he went limp, she dragged his body to the street and hung him from a tree just in front of the vacant house for everyone to see and left a note attached to his dead chest that read: *"Here comes the worst lawyer ever."*

Twenty

෴

Angel and Steven Blake

Angel returned to California after three weeks in Chicago. It relieved her to get a good night's rest. Exhausted from the trip, she took a shower and went to bed. Angel awoke the following day and prepared breakfast for herself and her Baby Girl. Her phone rang while they were eating breakfast. She checked the caller ID and confirmed that it was Steven.

Angel picked up the phone. *"Hi, Steven."*

"Good morning, Angel. What are your plans for today?"

"I had planned on taking my Baby Girl to the zoo, and after that, we are going to have lunch at McDonald's."

"Oh, that sounds like a plan. Well, I'm working today, and if you are free later, I would love to come and visit my best two girls today, if you don't mind." Steven sounded enthusiastic.

"Well, I'll call you when we get back home. I have to go, Steven. I'll talk to you later." Then Angel hung up.

Angel and her Baby Girl walked out the door after hanging up with Steven. She didn't want Steven to come over. Angel wanted to put some space between them. She was pushing her daughter through the zoo when she heard footsteps behind her. As she turned around to see who it was, it was this tall, dark, and handsome man dressed for the occasion. He smelled good enough to eat.

He looked at Angel and smiled. *"Slow down, sexy lady. I've been following you since you entered the zoo. Hi, my name is Wallace."*

"Oh, I'm sorry. My name is Angel, and this is my daughter, and her name is Gloria. She's a cutie."

"I was wondering if I could take you to beautiful ladies out to lunch?"

"Well, you could take us: but I will drive my car, okay? So I would follow you." Angel looked down at Gloria, who nodded with approval.

Angel drove to McDonald's as she promised with her daughter. When she pulled up at McDonald's, Wallace didn't have second thoughts. He just looked at the situation like this benefited the baby.

Angel thanked Wallace for lunch and said she'd see him later when she left McDonald's.

Wallace made sure he would see Angel again. *"Hold on a minute, baby. Can I get your seven digits before you go?"*

"Maybe we can do this again real soon."

Angel replied with a poker face. *"Sure, we can hook up sometime when you're not too busy with your woman."*

"Oh, it's not like that I have a girl, but we're on the outs right now, but it's all good."

"My woman is not the problem. I am." Wallace assured Angel.

Angel smiled because she admired his swagger and bravado. He was her type of guy. He was rough around the edges, so she knew he was a keeper.

Angel arrived home and bathed her daughter before putting her down for a much-needed nap. When her doorbell rang, Angel went into her living room, put on some Luther Vandross, and sang along to his songs. She thought to herself; *I wonder who the hell is ringing my doorbell like they crazy.* But when Angel peered through her door's peephole, she saw Steven, and it disgusted her. He showed up at her house without first calling. Angel was furious.

"What are you doing here, Steven? You just can't come to my home without calling." With Angel raising her voice slightly.

"Angel, I didn't mean no disrespect. I just thought that I would come by and surprise you, that's all. I went and bought the baby a few things that I thought she would like." Steven tried to diffuse the situation.

"Steven, first, never come to my house without calling again, and second, of all, my daughter has more stuff than any child I know. Thanks for thinking about her, anyway. I appreciate the thought." Angel dismissed the conversation right away.

Steven didn't like the fact that Angel snapped at him. He wanted her to emphasize that he was the one who made it possible for her to have a place to call home. When Angel noticed Steven's expression on his face, she knew he harbored some ill feelings, but Steven said nothing, so she didn't press what he was thinking. Angel's phone rang while she was sitting in the living room with Steven. When Angel heard the deep voice on the other end, she picked up the receiver and said hello. Angel recognized Wallace on the other line.

Wallace broke the ice. *"What's up, sexy lady? What's the agenda for today?"*

"Whatever you want to do." A smile broke out on Angel's face.

"Damn, I like your style. So let me get your address, and I'll call you before I come your way. Right now, I'm at my cousin's house recording my demo."

"Oh, so you can sing for sure?" Angel tried to be playful with her question.

Wallace wanted to impress Angel with his confidence. *"Sweetie, I can blow."*

"All right, Wallace, I will see you later on. Call me when you get ready to holler at me, okay?" Angel was trying hard not to show her excitement.

Steven looked like he'd swallowed a canary when Angel hung up the phone with Wallace. He wanted to know who Angel talked over the phone.

Steven was furious at Angel. Wallace intrigued him so much. *"Who's Wallace?"*

"First, I don't owe you an explanation of who I'm talking to. That is none of your business. Second, you're not my man. Remember, you were my

attorney, and now you better watch what you say to me because you, my brother, are treading on thin ice."

Steven was so enraged when he left Angel's house that he decided it was time to look into this Wallace character because he didn't want anyone interfering between him and Angel.

He thought to himself, *I've invested a lot of time in you and have poured out my feelings to you about how I feel about you, so I'm not about to let any want to be player or drug dealer take my woman away from me.*

That night, Steven called Angel to see if she was home, but when he didn't get an answer, he drove over to her house and sat down on the street to see who she was with. Steven waited for Angel and Wallace outside when she returned home. When they arrived, Wallace carried Angel's daughter inside and placed her on the couch.

Steven followed Wallace home after he left Angel's place. It intrigued him who this hood nigger was attempting to roll up on his woman. Steven did not know Wallace was a real thug; he was just a hustler who dropped niggers just for looking at him funny.

Steven called Angel to explain his feelings for her one more time. Angel answered the phone and told him to come over because she had some things to discuss with him. Angel was waiting for him at the front door when he arrived. As he entered the front door, Angel simply bowed her head; she needed to clear the air with Steven.

Angel tried to be as civil to Steven as possible. *"Do you want anything to drink before we start our conversation?"*

"Sure. Can I have a bottle of water? That would be fine." He said.

Angel went into her kitchen and got two bottles of water, and they headed to the living room to sit down.

Angel spoke and didn't want to beat around the bush. *"Look, you and I are just friends. Yes, we slept together a couple of times, and we both had a sexual enjoyment out of it, but now that the thrill is gone, so am I. I've moved on, and you need to do the same. We can remain friends, but that thing with friends with benefits is history. I've dealt you my last card."*

What Angel had just said to Steven had blown him out of the water. He was angry enough to spit in her face, but he knew doing so would be death. So he left Angel's house with hatred in his heart and murder in his mind. Angel couldn't care less that Steven was upset with her because she knew it would come to that one day, and she was more than willing to put his ass to rest.

If I couldn't have Angel, Wallace wouldn't get her either, Steven thought. Steven even thought that if he murdered her, he would adopt her daughter as his own. But, while Steven was contemplating killing Angel, she was thinking the same thing. Angel decided the day Steven left her house that it was well pastime to put Steven Blake to sleep. He'd worked her to the bone, and now it was time for him to kiss the world goodbye.

Angel had planned a kidnapping scheme for Steven. She wanted to call him and ask him to meet her for one last roll in the hay. Angel knew he couldn't pass up the chance to sleep with her. She exactly did what she was thinking. She called Steven, and he bolted.

Steven had a plan to choke Angel out while they were having sex, but he didn't realize Angel had her own plan. Angel had already reserved a room for them at the Hilton. She also hired a female hooker who resembled her. Angel went into the closet to hide while they were in the room. She had already gone to the room to arrange things. She had candles lit up all over the place. The hotel room was pitch black, with only candlelight illuminating the space.

Angel made sure that no one noticed her sneaking into the hotel. She had a silencer on her 38 caliber snug nose. She even brought her switch-blade in case anything went wrong. Angel's impersonator was already at the hotel by the time Steven came. She sprawled on the bed, naked. A few moments later, Steven knocked on the door.

"*Come in, Steven. The door is open,*" Steven heard her muffled voice from inside of the hotel room.

Steven entered the room and saw a naked body lying on the bed.

"*I hope you haven't started without me,*" he said.

"*No, baby, I was just waiting for you to arrive, but now that you're here, I don't want to wait any longer. So come over here baby, my body is heated. Let's get this party going.*" Her sultry voice barely echoed the room.

Steven had bought a bottle of red wine. *"Can I open our bottle of wine first?"*

"Sure, the glasses are on the table," she signaled Steven to pour some.

He popped the bottle and poured them a glass of wine. The dark crimson liquid sparkled in the candlelight. Steven took off his clothes and slid between the sheets. He pulled Angel's look-alike on top of him and kissed her with his eyes closed. He never opened his eyes once to see who really was on top of him.

"Roll over, baby, I want to hit it from behind," Steven changed position as he broke the kiss.

She rolled over, and Steven began talking to her, *"Are you sure you want all this meat to go to waste knowing you can have it for as long as you want?"*

Angel stormed out of the bathroom just as the impersonator was about to respond. *"Take your dick out slowly, turn around, and move over to the chair,"* she instructed Steven.

Angel tied him up with his dick still hanging when he did.

Angel moved over to the bed where her look-alike was sitting. Angel looked at her with an icy gaze. *"Good job, but I can't leave any witnesses."* And she stuck her thirty-eight in her mouth and blew her head off. Blood splattered all over the hotel wall.

After killing her doppelganger, Angel went back over to the chair where she had Steven tied up. She took off her pants.

"I'm going to give you a ride of your life before I kill you because, in reality, you have some good dick, but don't worry, I'm going to make it quick. You can bust your last nut because I'm taking your family jewels with me to keep as a reminder of how good you were in bed. I want you to know that when I meet up with Wallace tonight, I'm going to rock his world, and you can take that to the bank." Angel spoke with no trace of remorse in her voice.

Angel had her pistol up to Steven's head the entire time she was riding him to an orgasm. Finally, she pulled the trigger and shot Steven in the right temple of his head after she had her orgasm, and he just dropped his head to the side and took his last breath. Steven died, just like that.

Twenty-One

Angel and The Columbian Mafia

Ramon was sitting talking with his uncles when they mentioned Angel's name. One of his uncles wanted to hire Angel as their personal assassin because she was a skilled female assassin. She moved through the night as if it were darkness. They wanted Ramon to invite Angel to visit Columbia because they wanted to know more about her. They also wanted Angel to be a part of their organization.

Ramon wasn't sure if Angel would take their offer. He wanted Angel to be his wife, but not the way she was. She'd have to go through a lot of transformations before Ramon could consider her as wife material. He knew well Angel was lethal and not the one to play with. She murdered her entire mafia family and at least twenty Russians from the Russian mafia family.

Baby Girl is a hot commodity at the moment. She has a lot on her plate, but Ramon's idea would take some of the weight off her shoulders. That way, she can devote some time to him.

He dialed Angel's number at the request of his uncles, and to his surprise, Angel accepted. Angel, too, wanted to see Ramon. She hadn't seen him since he had left Chicago, and her body yearned for his touch. Angel and Ramon had never slept together, but Angel had an unwavering desire that her trip would not be a waste of time. Angel was about to find out what Ramon was thinking.

Ramon called Angel again while she was on a date with Wallace. She excused herself from the table and told Wallace she had to take the call.

She went outside to talk to Ramon, *"Are you ready to come to Columbia to visit me?"* His voice sounded enthusiastic.

Angel felt excited. *"Yes. When do you want me to come?"*

"What about tomorrow? I can pay for your ticket, or I could fly out on our private plane to get you." Ramon could hardly hide his desire to see Angel as soon as possible.

"Well, I tell you, what you can do is come pick me up on your private plane. That would be even better." Angel playfully requested.

"It's not a problem. I will be there in the morning around ten, and I will have my driver drive me to your house to pick you and your daughter up. How's that?" Ramon said without hesitation.

"It's a plan. I'm going home right now to pack our things." Angel was also eager to see Ramon.

Ramon asked, *"Aren't you at home right now?"*

"No. I'm on a date with this guy I just met. He seems all right for now, but he's not my guy or anything. So we are just kicking for now."

"All right, but cut your visit short with your friend and go home and pack," Ramon stated.

"All right," Angel said, and they hung up.

The next day, Ramon was at Angel's house on time. He was standing at Angel's door at ten-thirty. When Angel opened the door, she saw Ramon standing. She started smiling like a little schoolgirl.

Ramon's face lit up, *"What's up, ma? You ready to roll out?"*

"Of course, but I need to go into my room to get the suitcases."

Ramon looked at a man on his right. *"No. That's why I have my man Hotwire right here. Just show him where your room is, and he will take them to the car."*

Hotwire went and got the bags, put them in the car, and they were on their way to Columbia.

Angel was delighted to be in Ramon's company. Whatever he said didn't matter because she quietly had a mad crush on Ramon, but she thought he wasn't interested in her.

Ramon would not tell Angel that he had moved past the crush stage and had emotional feelings for her. Instead, he was going to show her how much she meant to him now that she was on his turf, and he wanted to lavish Angel's body from head to toe. He wanted to drink her juices and swallow her whole, but that would have to wait until his uncles had finished with Angel. But Ramon couldn't take his gaze away from her. She was stunning to him, and he knew his uncles would admire her as well.

All three of Ramon's uncles kissed Angel's hand as she walked into Ramon's Uncle Study. They all greet her with a big smile. Ramon's uncles thought she was dazzling and would be the perfect assassin. However, they had to get her to cross over to their organization first. They let her get comfortable before getting down to business, and they could tell their nephew had feelings for her, so they let him work his magic on her first.

Ramon talked so sweet and sexy to Angel that the only thing she could think of was, *Damn, he's sexy.* They went for a walk on the beach while the housekeeper cared for Angel's daughter. Ramon had the chef prepare a small snack for them, along with a bottle of white wine. He had a blanket laid out on the sand for them to sit on. She wished she could wrap her legs around his waist and let it do its thing. But Ramon would not let it go that easily. He wanted Angel in his bed, not on the sand at the beach where everyone could see her. She meant more to him than just a fuck.

Angel had drunk so much wine that she couldn't recall returning to Ramon's estate. She mistook them for still being on the beach. Ramon returned Angel to his estate. He undressed her and put her to bed in his guest room after she passed out from all the wine she had consumed. Ramon didn't want to make love to Angel while she was intoxicated. He wanted her to be sober so she would recognize him when he entered her private garden.

Angel woke up with a rocking headache, so she asked the maid for aspirin. Angel could hear her Baby Girl laughing, and she wondered who was making her laugh so hard. Before she could force herself to stand, Ramon entered the room with the baby on his shoulder, and they both grinned from ear to ear. It relieved her to see Ramon showing an interest in her daughter.

Ramon invited Angel to breakfast downstairs. Angel said she was going to take a quick shower and would be right down. Angel almost cried when she got downstairs to breakfast because they set the table up precisely like the Salvador's. Angel was sick to her stomach because everything she remembered about them was a lie.

Ramon sat next to Angel, and he kissed her forehead.

"It's all right, ma. I got you from here on out, and no one is going to make you second-rate again."

Angel smiled because, if nothing else, she knew Ramon felt something for her, but she wasn't sure if it was love yet, and she would not trust her heart too quickly this time. She wanted it to play out naturally because time would tell.

After Ramon and Angel finished eating breakfast, they were to meet Ramon's uncle to talk business. It concerned Angel because she did not know what these Columbian mafia kingpins wanted from her. Angel was taken aback when Ramon's uncle Leo told her he wanted her to join their organization as a female assassin. She had never considered herself to be an assassin. She had always thought of herself as a murderer, but putting a name to it was hilarious.

Angel couldn't believe what they'd just said. She had to ask. *"Why me?"*

"Because no one would ever expect you because you come in the night like a ghost, and we never had a female in our organization that was heartless like yourself." Uncle Leo said with a firm tone.

"If I take your offer, what will be my job as your personal assassin?" Angel looked skeptical.

Uncle Leo stood up and said. *"You will be on call to hit wherever we want you, so this means you would be on call twenty-four hours a day."*

"My price would be a half-million dollars a job, and if I have to go out of state, I would need your plane to get me there, and my daughter comes first, no ifs and buts about it," Angel said to Uncle Leo.

"If my daughter becomes ill or injured and requires my attention, I will

be there for her. Everything else is incidental. Do we have an agreement? Otherwise, I'm backing out this organization right now."

Ramon's uncle looked at Angel with a smile, and everyone else in the room followed suit. Angel was tough, but they agreed to her terms, and Angel became the female assassin for the Columbian mafia.

Twenty-Two

～

Angel: The Columbian Lady Assassin

Angel was officially a female assassin hired by the Columbian mafia. Ramon flew her back home to California after a week in Columbia.

Angel was off to bed when her phone rang; it was Wallace.

He called Angel while in Columbia, but she did not answer or return his calls, which worried him. Finally, when Angel answered the phone, he was happy to hear her voice.

"I am fine, and my phone doesn't have any reception where I was."

"Okay, but can I ask where you went?"

Angel hates it when men ask questions about her personal space.

"I'm sorry, but I don't like 21 questions. I'm not your woman, and you're not mine. If I don't ask your whereabouts, don't ask mine. You just woke me up from a peaceful sleep to question me."

"I just wanted to make sure you were okay. I'll call you tomorrow if that's fine with you, ma."

Angel replied before Wallace could finish his sentence.

"Goodnight, Wallace. I'll talk with you tomorrow, all right?"

"Okay," and Angel hung up, leaving Wallace with the phone still in his ear.

Wallace hated how Angel was treating him like a little punk, so the next time he saw her, he'd put her in her place. But he did not know what Angel could do.

Wallace couldn't sleep because he couldn't stop thinking about how Angel shut him down. No female had looked down at him before, but Angel had him twisted.

Angel was on her way out when she heard car wheels screeching in her driveway.

"I know this nigger would show up at my place unannounced. He must want me to put two hollow points in his head."

Wallace jumped out of his car, grabbed Angel by the arm, and dragged her back inside the house, almost dropping her daughter, which triggered Angel into a rage that it did not prepare him for.

Angel lost her control. She put her daughter down and went to the kitchen, grabbed a butcher knife, and started stabbing Wallace so fast he hit the floor. She was still stabbing him with the knife as she knelt. Angel didn't stop until he couldn't breathe.

She looked at Wallace and said, *"Don't mess with my daughter, Nigger, and I should have told you, sucker, I'm a killer."*

"Damn, now someone got to bury this fool."

So she wrapped him in plastic and dragged him into his car's trunk. She will take him behind a building that she'd passed one day. They had concrete mixing equipment, so she thought it would be a good place because they won't smell his ass when he stinks.

Angel smiled as she left the cement grave, pleased with herself for another notch on her belt. Her phone rang as she was on her way to get some food.

It was Uncle Leo. He had an assignment for her. She needed to go home to get the information he sent while she was away. He had pictures of the guy he wanted Angel to kill. That guy owed the family $200,000. He knew they were looking for him, so he skipped town.

When Angel returned home, she discovered the envelope. She put her daughter to bed, got a drink, and opened the envelope to see who the person was. When she saw the man's picture,

"Oh my god," she thought to herself, "I would have done this one for free."

The picture she saw was Judge Baker.

"I'm going back to Chicago quicker than I thought, so I might as well kill two birds with one stone."

Angel was ready to return to Chicago on Friday. Judge Baker was her next target. She took a shower in her loft and went to Club Sexy.

The club was jumping when she entered. She spotted Judge Baker in his usual location. Angel knew the man liked it whenever an attractive woman did weird things to him, so she had that pan covered.

Angel made her way over to his table.

"Do you want to go upstairs to VIP with me?"

He said, *"Yes. Is there a room up there with a door?"*

"Of course, there is handsome. Are you ready to go?"

The Judge jumped up and headed to the stairs.

When Angel and the Judge made it upstairs, she asked him,

"What do you want me to do for you, handsome?"

"I want you to take my belt off and spank me with it."

"Is there anything else you prefer me to do?"

Judge Baker immediately answered,

"Yes, I want you to take the heel of your shoe and step on my balls with it, and then I want you to light this candle and pour the hot wax down the crack of my ass."

Angel left the room and went to the restroom. She wanted him to remember her as Angel Carter.

She had her pistol strapped to her thigh and went back to their room.

"Can I get down and freak with you?"

"Come on with it. I can handle whatever you throw at me."

That was right up Angel's alley. She had guns, switchblades, duct tape, and a jar of battery acid in her purse. She was going to make the Judge pay for sending her to the hellhole of a prison.

Angel drugged the Judge's drink. He started slurring, so she laid him back on the bed and used her switchblade to cut off his eyelids. She wanted him to see everything she was going to do to him.

"You don't remember me, do you? I'm Angel Carter, the threat to Chicago."

The Judge could do nothing but jump on the bed because Angel had him bound with duct tape. He knew she was going to kill him.

"I'll make this quick, Your Honor. Don't worry, the pain will be like re-moving a bandage. You'll die immediately."

She loaded a needle with liquid Amtrak and injected it into the Judge, who instantly swelled up like the size of a basketball.

Angel left the room without looking back. She had one more victim to get rid of before leaving Chicago.

She went to meet up with the next on her hit list, Judge O'Malley.

Angel made a call to Judge O'Malley to meet her at Motel 6. She said she was a call girl that needed his attention.

Judge O'Malley asked her a few questions.

"How do I know you, and where did you get my number?"

"From the agency you used to get private shows."

"I know what you are talking about. I'll be there around eight."

"I will be here in room 312 on the third floor."

"Who should I ask for, Crystal?"

"Yes"

"All right. Crystal, see you then."

Judge O'Malley arrived at the room disappointed, because he had never been in a run-down hotel before. He was going to get his freak on and go home to his wife, but he didn't know he'd never see Mrs. O'Malley again.

Angel asked Judge O'Malley,

"What is your specialty of the night?"

"I want a bathtub full of Jell-O and a spoon so I could eat some while I'm relaxing."

After he got out of the tub, he commanded Angel,

"I want you to spread some whipped cream on my genitals and lick them slowly."

Angel said, "All right, Your Honor, your wish is my command."

Angel told the Judge she had to go into the bedroom to get him a gift. She returned with a blowtorch. The Judge looked up at Angel as if lightning struck him.

"Judge O'Malley, this is your chance to repent. You need to hurry because you have little time left."

The Judge was in tears.

"Please don't kill me. I have a wife and three children."

"That's funny because if your wife meant that much to you, your freaky ass wouldn't be here sitting in a bathtub of Jell-O to get fried with a blowtorch."

That scared the Judge more because Angel aimed the blow torch right at him. His skin was frying like chicken in hot grease.

Angel left the hotel satisfied. She had killed two birds with one stone. She headed back to her loft, took a shower, and then went to bed.

The following day, she drove back to California. She still had an army of targets on her list, so she planned to return to Chicago later to finish what she had started.

When she made it back home, another envelope was under her door. She looked at it and threw it on the table.

Angel couldn't sleep, so she stood up, grabbed the envelope from the table, and opened it. She saw pictures of two Russian guys. One of them was Boris, the head of the Russian mafia, and the other was Boris's brother, the second man in command.

Uncle Leo wanted the Russian mafia out of his way as they kept interfering with his shipments, and he had trucks going through Russia. Those mafias would kill every man that was from Columbia.

Ramon had Angel's back, sent her a passport, and provided her with all information she needed to set up a camp in Russia. She just needed someone to take care of her daughter because there was no way she was taking her to Russia. So, she sent Mary, their housekeeper, to watch Angel's daughter while she's away. Angel trusted Mary because she spent a lot of time with her Baby Girl in Columbia.

Mary had made it to California, so it was time for Angel to take the flight to Russia.

Ramon had sent Angel to a lovely village in Russia. He made sure she had all the weapons she needed. Angel was ready to blow up Russia if necessary, armed with missiles, hand grenades, guns, and even C4.

Angel stayed in her room during the day and moved into the night like a ninja. She would plant C4 around the Russian compound to make sure the destruction of the entire Russian mafia family. Angel buried herself in a dirt hole she dug outside the compound and had all of her weapons in hand, so she could kill anyone who came out of the compound after she blew it up. She would do anything to finish the job and get out of Russia.

The night Angel lit the compound up was like the Fourth of July. People were trying to escape the fire, but Angel wouldn't let anyone get away. Four men were running out of the compound, with their bodies on fire. She emerged from the dirt hole, drew her weapon, and slashed their heads off.

Mission accomplished. Angel got herself together and headed back to the airport, but when she arrived, she couldn't leave.

The Russian police had the airport locked down so that no one could leave Russia.

She called Ramon and told him,

"Job's all done, but there's no way I could leave Russia by plane. So I have to use Plan B to set off the explosion to blow up half of Russia."

"I'm on my way."

Ramon told his pilot to fuel up. They were going to Russia to pick up Angel. Uncle Leo told them to be careful and to fly under the radar. Angel fled the airport quickly, knowing she would meet Ramon and the pilot on high ground. So, she had to get to the top end of Russia.

After eight hours, they picked her up, unharmed, and two million dollars richer.

Twenty-Three

~

Angel's Killing Spree in Chicago

Angel was glad to be out of Russia. She wiped out another mafia family. Angel went home to her daughter and planned to rest before returning to the Windy City.

She was watching the news when she saw a woman crying, saying her husband had gone missing for two months. The woman described her husband and showed a photo of him.

When Angel saw the picture, she thought to herself,

"Lady, you'll never see that son of a bitch husband again. I buried your husband Wallace in a concrete grave two months ago."

Angel felt uneasy. She wanted more blood spilled, so she decided it was time to return to Chicago. Angel returned to Chicago and went to her restaurant.

She noticed two of her men while eating in the sugar shack. Angel's men dismantled when she went to jail. Angel had no plans to regroup her troops. She didn't need help because she was a one-woman killing machine.

Angel was at home when she felt uneasy. She wanted more blood spilled, so she decided it was time to return to Chicago.

Angel entered Chicago and went to her restaurant, The Sugar Shack.

She was eating when she noticed two of her men. Angel's men dismantled when she went to jail. Angel had no plans to regroup her troops. She didn't need help because she was a one-woman killing machine.

When Angel sat at the table behind them, she heard Mia's name come up. She really wanted to know what they were talking about.

So when she heard them say Mia wanted to kill her for killing Mia's brother, St. Louis, she had to add Mia's name to her hit list.

Angel decided to kill Hammer first, her brother's right-hand man, for testifying at her trial. Especially since he was put into their organization as a police informant.

She wanted his head, and he won't get away that easily. But, of course, Angel knew precisely where to find Hammer now that he's retired.

It was a piece of cake for her, especially because she heard he was hanging out at Thigh High bar, where women have big thighs?

Angel went to Thigh High bar, and when she walked in, she overheard a guy whispering who she was. After that, people at the club quickly figured out who she was.

Angel ordered rounds for everyone, including women in the club. She made sure the bartender kept them coming.

Angel wanted everyone in the club to get drunk because she didn't want anyone to remember her snatching Hammer's big ass out of the club.

Angel waited until Hammer passed out in the booth in which he was sitting. Then she woke him up and asked if he wanted to go have some fun with her. She even let him rub her ass.

Hammer looked at Angel and said. *"You damn skippy, I want to have some fun with you. My truck is parked at the back."*

We can do whatever you want in there. *"My seats recline all the way, and I have tinted windows, so no one can see inside my truck. So, come on, baby girl, let's go burn some rubber."*

Angel waited until Hammer got undressed inside his truck. She then covered his eyes with a scarf and handcuffed him to the steering wheel.

After that, Angel took his blackjack and started beating Hammer to death with his own nightstick.

"This is what you get for being a snitch and a trader," she said to Hammer.

Hammer was so out of it, he couldn't comprehend what Angel was saying. She beat Hammer in the head so hard that his eyeballs popped out, and his nose was on the left side of his face. He would need a closed-casket funeral because his face and head were completely disfigured.

Angel wasn't done yet. She'd moved on to her next victim, the Commissioner.

He tried to rape Angel in her cell while locked up in the back, waiting to be transported to the women's prison. He would have raped her if it weren't for the female Sheriff.

The Sheriff walked in and called Angel's name right on time. The Commissioner looked at Angel and said.

"Next time we're alone, I'm going to rip your asshole. So keep that in mind, Ms. Carter."

Angel couldn't understand what the Commissioner said that day. She kept replaying what he said in her head like a scratched CD, but she had to make him pay for being so stupid.

She thought to herself. How could you rape a prisoner while she was waiting to be transported to another jail? She knew he was a sick man, but she would make sure his sickness never reached another female on lockdown.

Angel was sitting in her car at a red light when the Commissioner's car stopped beside her. She thought to herself. *"This must be my lucky day. This asshole is about to meet his maker sooner than I expected."*

Angel let the Commissioner pull off first so she could follow him. When she saw him pulled off to a house on an old street, Mia came to the door wrapped in a towel.

Angel said. *"Yes, this is my lucky day. I don't have to go looking for this bitch. She was exactly where she needed to be."*

Angel went around the back of the house and slid in through the basement window. She landed on top of a pile of dirty clothes on the basement floor. She stopped for a moment and laughed because Mia was an inconsequential woman.

Angel was climbing the basement stairs when she heard screams. She peeped through the crack in the door and saw the Commissioner choking the dog shit out of Mia.

Angel told herself. *"Kill the bitch, and once you're done with her, it's your turn, you crazy ass pervert."*

The Commissioner stopped choking Mia because he heard something. He let go of Mia, and she dropped to the floor like an old rag doll. He went to the kitchen because he thought the noise came from there. When he turned around and went back to choke Mia, Angel came out from behind the basement door and hit the Commissioner in the head with a bat she found in the basement, knocking him out.

When the Commissioner woke up, he was tied to the bed, right beside Mia. Angel slapped Mia to wake her up so she would know why she would kill her. Angel told Mia and the Commissioner that they wouldn't live to see daylight.

"You might as well be still because when I tie a knot, you can't make it lose," Angel said, as Mia squirmed.

The Commissioner looked to see if she was really Angel Carter. Still, he couldn't see the resemblance because Angel had plastic surgery on her face, contact lenses, changed hair color, and everything.

"Do you know the game operation, dumbass?" Angel asked the Commissioner.

He said, *"Yeah."*

"Good, because I'm going to operate on both of you," Angel said.

Mia started screaming loud when she said that, so Angel had to cover her mouth with socks and tape.

"I think I'm going to start with you first," Angel told the Commissioner. Then she put her handbag on the bed and pulled out a machete.

She hit the Commissioner right in the middle of his chest with it, then took out his heart and put it in a plastic bag.

Then Angel stalled on Mia.

"I always admired the color of your eyes, she told Mia. So I think I will take your eyeballs out and mail them to your son. You think I knew nothing about you, huh? Your son's name is Shawn, isn't it?"

"Yes, but please don't put my son through that kind of trauma. Please, Angel. He has nothing to do with any of this."

"You should have thought about your son being traumatized when you crossed me, but you know I will give you the honor of calling your son one last time before I put you to sleep," Angel said.

Angel gave Mia a phone to call her son. She was crying, and her twelve-year-old son asked her, *"Why are you crying, mommy?"*

"Because I love you, and I always will." She said.

Angel told Mia to hang up the phone and say goodnight to her son, which would be the last time he would hear his mother's voice.

Angel electrocuted Mia, and after she took her last breath, Angel removed Mia's eyeballs and put them in a plastic bag with the Commissioner's heart.

Angel was about to leave Mia's house when she realized she couldn't leave their bodies lying out like that. So she went into the garage, got the gas can, poured gas all over the house, and set it on fire. Then she left Mia's house the same way she came in, through the basement window.

Angel loved the way blood felt in her hands every time she killed someone. She felt a surge of energy. It made her heart pump hard, and she liked the excitement it gave her.

She finished her job in Chicago, and everyone involved in her case was dead.

She had two more people to destroy, but Angel just wanted to sit back and let nature take its course on those two because she knew her two friends, Abby and Gabriel, would wait for her. So she let them watch their backs for a while, knowing that if she came for them in the shadows of the night, they wouldn't even notice.

Twenty-Four

The One Woman - Killing Machine

Angel was in Columbia for an assignment and was supposed to be there for the next three weeks. However, she had to travel to Delaware to meet a guy named Paul Adams in two days. Angel checked into the Holiday Inn when she arrived in Delaware.

Paul was the owner of The Vault, the hottest club in the Delaware area. He had pole dancers, strippers, and even rooms in the back of his club where mixed couples orgies. Every door is guarded.

Paul used to be a pimp, and he dressed as if he were still in the seventies. He imagined himself to be every woman's dream and every man's nightmare. Paul held enough jewelry to choke a horse and treated his women as if they were God's gift to men.

Paul was supposed to be running that part of the town for the Columbians. However, he despised the Columbians and thought he would be ready when they sent their men to come for him if he took their money and fled town. He didn't realize that they had already sent someone for him and what he loved the most was what would take his ass out there.

Angel rented a Rolls-Royce with GPS so she could pinpoint Club Vault's location. When she walked through the doors, all eyes were on her. Angel donned an all-white leather gown with the back cut out down to her tailbone. She had the white Armani and white boots to match, with two pearl-white forty-fives attached to her side beneath her white fur coat. Angel came prepared for whatever jumped off.

She went to the bar and ordered a Cognac with a glass of water to get a feel of Vault Club. After that, she went to the restroom twice to look for escape routes. Angel wasn't concerned about Paul's bodyguards. She could have them eat at her palms like little puppies.

Angel had been sitting in Vault Club for an hour, and she still hadn't spotted Paul yet. She knew what he looked like because she had a picture of him. Another hour passed, and two more cognacs. Paul came through the door sporting a white mink coat with two white chicks on his arm. Angel was damn near drunk because she thought Paul's ugly ass was okay. She said to herself. *Shake this shit off because there's my victim right there, so let me get to work.*

While Paul was standing at the bar, Angel stood up to use the restroom once more. She knew he peered at her when he walked in the door, so Angel knew if she made eye contact with him, he'd want to know who she was. Paul asked his bartender what she was drinking and got her another one on him. When Angel returned to her seat, the bartender handed her another drink.

"Excuse me, I didn't order another drink," Angel called out to the bartender.

The bartender pointed down to the end of the bar where Paul was standing, holding up his drink. He was looking at Angel and waving his hand for her to come and join him.

Angel stood up and walked to the far end of the bar, where Paul was. He drew out the barstool and invited Angel to take a seat. Paul extended his hand out to introduce himself to Angel. She presented herself as Jennifer.

"That's a beautiful name for a beautiful woman." Paul was slightly caressing her hand.

Angel looked at him, smiling. *"Thank you."*

They shared two more drinks before Paul invited Angel to his office upstairs. Angel didn't mind going to Paul's office because she knew she could take his life wherever she wanted.

Paul and Angel were sitting in his office when he told Angel he had to drain the dragon.

"Sure, go ahead." Angel nodded with approval.

While Paul was out of the office, Angel took her guns and tucked them behind her back, out of sight of Paul. Paul was so intoxicated that he wouldn't even see a snake crawling on the floor. The music was blaring so loudly that no one would hear Angel's forty-fives going off. Besides, she had silencers on both of them and hollow-point bullets loaded as well.

Paul got straight to the point with Angel. *"Damn, baby, I want to see what you are working with under that coat."*

"Only if you let me see what you are working inside your pants," Angel smirked, glancing at Paul's crotch.

Paul looked at Angel seductively. *"I'm working with a monster. Baby, you might not handle all of this."*

Paul took his pants off and lo-and-behold; his dick was so long and thick. Angel couldn't believe her eyes. All she could mutter was, *"Damn."*

Angel's job was to kill the man, but when she saw Paul's meat, she wanted to have some, so she sat on Paul's lap and rode him like a bronco bull. Paul said it was the best piece of ass he had in a long time. He was so exhausted that Angel jumped off his lap, grabbed her forty-five, stuck it in his mouth, *"Never trust a bitch with a gun."* Angel also revealed to Paul that she was a Columbian assassin sent by Leo to kill him and that his time on Earth had ended.

Angel was walking down the stairs when one of Paul's bodyguards asked if Paul was still in his office. She told him he was in his restroom washing up.

She paused at the bar for a moment before exiting. Before Angel could get to the door, one bodyguard started screaming, *"Hold that bitch!"* Angel swung back her coat and came up with her twins. The forty-fives were blazing before the other bodyguards could get close to her. She had hit about twenty people before she stopped shooting. Angel was unharmed because the bodyguards didn't even have time to draw their weapons. Angel was ruthless with pistol play; she had the Club Vault smoking.

That night, Angel checked out of the Holiday Inn. She brought the Rolls-Royce she rented to a different town and returned it there. Angel didn't think she could easily kill Paul, but she knew men wouldn't turn down a known ass, which is where he fucked up. He should have kept it moving, but he wanted to stick his dick in something hot, and it was what got him dead.

Angel returned to Columbia on time. She'd completed another hit. She was glad to see her Baby Girl laugh again. Angel was in the room with her daughter when they heard a knock on the door.

Angel didn't bother to open the door herself. *"Come in."* It turns out it was Uncle Leo.

Uncle Leo walked in and handed Angel $500,000 for the job she had just finished. He gave Angel another envelope containing images of three men he wanted her to execute. She asked Uncle Leo, *"When do I leave?"*

Uncle Leo didn't want to beat around the bush. *"At dawn."*

"I'll be ready. I just need to get more ammunition and some C4, too. So they won't remember what hit them this time." Angel told Uncle Leo.

Angel had Uncle Leo refuel the jet. She was on her way to Fresno, California, to carry out three hits. Her targets were the heads of the Crips and Bloods; Ace, Casper, and Buck. They had hits on them for killing Rickey, Uncle Leo's son. Rickey was in Fresco visiting his girlfriend Anita when Ace, who was also messing around with Anita, showed up at her house one night. The two men ended up in a gunfight. Ace shot Rickey in the head twice and died right on the spot. He sent Rickey's body into a wooden box back to Columbia. Uncle Leo took this as a threat to the Columbians, so Ace and his entire gang had to be exterminated.

Angel had carried enough ammunition with her to blow up Fresno. She even brought a powerful stun gun with her. Angel wanted to make a statement and make sure the guys on the West Coast knew the pressure she would put on their asses. However, the trip made her feel uneasy, so she just said to herself, *It would be perfectly fine.*

Angel arrived in Fresno and checked into the Sheraton Hotel. She rented a 2011 pearl-white Bentley and drove through Fresno, bumping her music to Gerald Levert's private-label CD *"School Me."* She used her GPS to pinpoint the location of the Crips and Bloods' spot at Imperial Street. Angel planned to hit their spot as soon as it got dark. She was driving down Imperial Street when she recognized her three targets. They were heavily guarded, so she told herself, *I'm not wasting my time. Everyone in the house has to go.*

Angel had some time before it got dark, so she pulled over at a restaurant and ordered something to eat. As she sat down at her table and was waiting for her food, she overheard men across her table arguing. Angel was astounded to see all three of her targets and at least six more men with them. She thought to herself, *Either these niggers are following me, or I'm tripping. But, of course, I'm going with the tripping part because they can't possibly believe I'm here to kill them.*

Angel got her food, but she kept feeling like someone was staring at her, so she looked up, and it was Casper. "Can I sit down?" he asked Angel as he approached her table.

Angel acted casual. *"Yes, it's a free country."*

"What's your name, beautiful?"

Angel answered him with a question. *"What's yours? You came over here interrupting my meal."*

"My name is Casper."

"Like Casper the Friendly Ghost?" Angel was trying to insert some humor.

"Yeah, something like that," Casper smirked.

"All right, Casper the Friendly Ghost, my name is Jenny, like I dream of Jennie."

Angel couldn't help but laugh. *"Oh, I see, you got jokes, all right. I like that you're not from around here."*

Angel looked amused. *"How do you know that?"*

"I run Fresno. I know everyone here, and there's no way I would have missed someone as fine as you are." Casper was now flirting with her.

The mind games did not faze Angel. *"Well, you missed me, player. I've been around for a while."*

"Oh, really, okay. Why is it I haven't seen you then because you didn't want to be seen?"

Angel had no plans on being picked up by Casper or anyone else in his crew. Her only focus was to set fire to their asses and return to Columbia as soon as it got dark enough for her to do her job. She wasn't even engaged in his conversation. It was a hit-or-miss situation with her. She wasn't interested, and everything he said just went right over her head.

Casper looked surprised by how Angel rejected him. *"Damn, ma, I never had a woman to give me such a cold shoulder. You do like men, don't you, ma?"*

"Of course, I love men. You just aren't the type of man I go for."

"Damn, ma, that was cold." Casper was a little embarrassed.

"No disrespect. I like men that wear belts to keep their pants up, not with their pants down to their ankles."

"All right, I feel you. So you telling me if I put a belt on and pull my pants up, I might have a shot with you?"

"No. What I'm saying is I like a man with class, that's all. Let me wrap this up real quick for you. I'm not interested in you, period." As soon as Angel said that, she quickly stood up and left.

Angel walked out of the restaurant without looking back, but she still had Casper's attention. He couldn't shake the feeling that Angel had turned him off. That never happened to him before, so it irritated him that his boys were teasing him about a girl as fine as Angel, who wanted no parts of him.

Angel made Casper second-guess himself because he was the finest one out of his whole crew.

Casper called out one of his crewmen, *"Something has to be wrong with that bitch. Don't know woman pass up a nigger like me. She must like pussy for real, dog. Look, check this out. We gonna forget about what just happened and stick to the job at hand. We are going to roll on these fools on the West Side. We know where their meth lab is and go in there and take their shit and roll out."*

Buck interrupted the conversation. *"Hold up, Casper. You talking crazy because them boys got some mad-fire powered up in there, so do we fool. So stop being a bitch and let's go. How about you, Ace? You ready or you tripping out too?"*

"No, I'm down for whatever, man, so let's make it do what it does."

Angel remained in the parking lot, watching their every move. They were so caught up in what they were doing they didn't notice Angel following closely behind them. Finally, they all put on their masks, kicked open the front door to the meth lab, and went inside. Angel sat across the street, watching everything unfold. She said to herself, *These niggers are gangsters, but not gangster enough because a true gangster will eliminate them—me. As soon as the sun goes down, I'm going to put their lights out.*

Angel returned to the Sheraton to retrieve her firearms, placed them in a duffel bag, and exited the building. She armed herself with everything from switchblades to Uzis and C4 explosives, ready as a backup. Angel returned to Imperial Street and sat there until it got dark, but this time she sat further down the street because they saw what she was driving. Angel's mind was working nonstop. She thought *I needed to take this car back to the hotel, park it, and steal a beat-up dark-colored ride.* So Angel drove back to the hotel, parked it, and then stole a black Impala from the hotel parking lot. *It wouldn't get as much attention as the pearl-white Bentley,* she thought.

Angel returned to Imperial Street and parked down the street. She scooted down in the seat so no one would notice a suspicious woman sitting in a car. It was quickly getting dark. Angel placed her explosives on the front seat to take out what she needed to blow up the house. She noticed two young boys enter the house. *Damn!* she exclaimed to herself. *I hope they go in and come out because I would hate to blow their little asses up in smoke with the rest of the clowns. I'm going to give them twenty minutes. After that, it's smoking time.*

Angel waited for twenty minutes. They didn't come out, so she had to do what she needed to do under different circumstances. If it had been a solo job, she would have given the little boys more time to come out. But it was all about money, and nothing or no one would stop her from getting her paper. Angel took two packages of C4 from her bag, as well as two Uzis. She had two 38-caliber snug nose pistols strapped to her side.

Angel crept up to the house. She placed all the C4 around the house. Angel detonated the explosives and ran into the bushes to hide. She was waiting for anyone to come out of the house alive when she set off the detonators, and then all hell broke loose. The house blew up in a tremendous explosion. She saw bodies flying like rag dolls. When she emerged from the bushes, she found herself face to face with Casper. Angel drew the Uzis and fired a barrage of rounds into Casper's body. He looked at Angel one last time before dying and falling into the grass. Angel had taken down the entire gang—another task completed.

Angel was driving home from Fresno when the realization of being a mother struck her like a bolt of lightning. She only has her daughter. Angel had a hunch about her daughter growing up without her mother's love and affection. She became engrossed in her work as an assassin and lost sight of the love that binds a mother and daughter. Her first instinct was to minimize her job as an assassin and only accept an assignment once a month. She planned to inform Uncle Leo of her agreement, and if he did not take her terms, she would have to decline to be their assassin.

Angel expressed her concerns to Uncle Leo and the other Columbians. They unanimously agreed as long as she remained their assassin. She had every right to spend time with her daughter. They understood the significance of family. Angel returned to California with her daughter to begin their mother-daughter relationship. She intended to raise her daughter the same way her history raised her. Angel wished to train Gloria as an assassin as well. Angel wanted them to be known as the mother and daughter assassins for the Columbian mafia.

Twenty-Five

~

Baby Girl in Training

Angel got up early to take her Baby Girl to her first shooting range training. Gloria was ecstatic to go. She had been pleading Angel for weeks, asking when it would be her turn to hold a gun. Angel explained how deadly firearms were. She wanted her daughter to be well-versed in all facets of assassination. She had to work her way up from the bottom, like how Angel's predecessors taught her. Angel put her Baby Girl through a two-year military training program, which was difficult for Baby Girl. However, she wanted it all; Baby Girl wanted to be her mother's shadow.

Angel even had her daughter wear military camouflage to show her that being an assassin was a serious business and that one mistake could lead to their deaths. She had Baby Girl undergo a year of mixed martial arts training before sending her out on a job as her backup. The mafia assigned Angel to St. Louis on a mission to assassinate Black, a.k.a. Danny Stone. He was in charge of St. Louis' West Side. He handled all of his operations all the way to the Central West End.

Black got his drugs from the Columbians and short-changed them with counterfeit money. His most recent shipment was $50,000 in pure uncut heroin. He dispatched The Sandman, his right-hand man, to Columbia to retrieve the package. The Sandman returned to St. Louis after handing over the money to the Columbians. They were furious when they discovered that The Sandman duped them into accepting phony money. The Columbians knew well that they had to deal with Black. Then they dispatched Angel, their personal assassin, into the fray.

It thrilled Angel to get an assignment because she would take her Baby Girl along as backup. She wanted to prime her for her first stint out of the gate. Angel and Baby Girl arrived in St. Louis early that morning. They arrived at the Hyatt Hotel in downtown St. Louis and checked in. Then she got in her car and used her GPS to find a street called Blackstone on the West Side of St. Louis. Angel pulled up at the intersection between Blackstone Street and Page Avenue, where she plotted her escape routes.

Angel and Baby Girl sat in her car, watching the traffic come and go from Black's drug house. She'd seen pictures of Black, but she had yet to see him. Then, Baby Girl started getting hungry and asked Angel how long they would sit out there before she got something to eat.

Angel gave her a quick reminder, *"Listen to me carefully. When you are stalking a target, you never leave your post unless it's daylight like it is now, or you got him locked in your sights so you can take him right out."*

Baby Girl understood what Angel was saying, and she decided she could eat later because they would be on their way back to California after they hit Black. Angel and Baby Girl stayed on the corner, watching Black's spot in a black tricked-out Charger with tinted windows, which did not sit well with one of Black's henchmen, Blaze. After about twenty minutes of sitting there, he noticed them. He called Black that either the police were watching them or niggers who wanted to rob his spot.

Black was at his apartment when he got the call from Blaze. He gave him the order to gather two more of his soldiers and run-up to the side of Angel's car, snatching them out of their ride and taking them to the dope house, where they would hold them until he arrived.

"No, better yet," Black had a better idea in mind. *"Let's keep going until it gets dark. You know, we already have people watching our block, so just relax for the time being. It'll be dark in an hour, so just be cool until then."*

Angel suspected that someone was watching her, so she left her post. She wanted to switch vehicles. Angel wanted a car that no one had seen sitting outside the dope house, so she went to steal a Buick. When Black called Blaze to check on the vehicle, he confirmed the car wasn't there anymore. Then, Black instructed Blaze to pack everything and move it down to their other dope house on Wells, where he would meet him in half an hour.

Blaze confirmed his instructions. *"Cool, I'll see you then."*

Black started sweating. He said to himself, *Something isn't right. Maybe those punk-ass Russians sent somebody to hit my ass, or maybe nigger Bo Pete we robbed last week and took all his shit, including the nigger's safe. That nigger Bo Pete is scary. He don't have the balls to come at me because he know what time it is.*

Angel followed Blaze to the dope house on Wells Street. He was so preoccupied with moving dope that he didn't notice the Buick following him. Angel and Baby Girl were preparing their munitions for what was about to happen. They armed themselves with two MAC-10s, four Uzis, and a few hand grenades. What Angel saw next was the icing on the cake. It was her intended target, Black. He showed up in a burgundy Yukon.

Angel looked at her daughter. *"There he is, right there. This is going to be short and sweet. We will be back home before the sun comes up."*

Angel urged her daughter to put on her camouflage uniform because it would be dark in a few minutes, and they were going in guns a-blazing. She didn't want to leave a single soul alive in that house. Angel extracted all the weaponry from the bag. She began securing the MAC-10s to her thigh. She handed Baby Girl two Uzis and two switchblades. It thrilled Baby Girl to be on her mother's first assignment.

Angel briefed Baby Girl she was entering through the front door and wanted her to meet her outside the back door, in the bushes. She wanted Baby Girl hiding in the bushes, firing at anyone who came out the back door. Angel kicked in the front door and started shooting. She emptied the magazine of her MAC-10 at Blaze until his body slammed the floor like a ton of bricks.

Angel tore the other four guys in the house to shreds. They were so high on heroin that they didn't even notice when she kicked the door in. When Black attempted to flee through the back door, Baby Girl shot him twice in the leg. He knelt on the ground, clutching his leg. She was under Angel's orders not to kill him, so she targeted him on the leg instead.

Angel was in the house when she heard gunshots coming from the back, so she ran to see if Baby Girl was okay. She grinned when she saw Baby Girl had Black pinned down because she had paid attention to her training. Angel told Black that she was going to take him on a little ride. He was gushing blood from his leg. Angel had a syringe full of heroin ready to put Black to sleep until she arrived at her next destination.

Angel found a vacant storefront building on Page Boulevard. She dragged Black inside the empty storefront after getting out of the car with her Baby Girl. He was still high on the heroin Angel had injected directly into his neck. Angel told Black to pay attention and wake up because she was only going to say it once. Angel ordered Baby Girl to go to the car and get her battery-powered saw. She was going to make certain that Black gave no one phony money again because his number was up.

Angel clutches Black's shirt. *"Why would you think the Columbians would be so stupid and not have their money checked?"*

Black was still groggy but talked back. *"Fuck the Columbians bitch, and fuck you too."*

"All right, let's see who gets fucked now, player." Angel then grabbed the battery-powered saw.

Angel turned on her battery-powered saw and began by chopping off both of Black's legs. He screamed so loudly that his voice echoed throughout the store. This startled a homeless man who was sleeping in the back. Angel had Baby Girl watch the front of the empty store so that if anyone passed by, she could warn her. The homeless man peered through a hole in the wall and witnessed Angel dismember Black with a saw. He became so terrified that he peed in his pants. The homeless man, Dirty Bob, Dirty Bob, a homeless man, jumped back so far that he knocked over a can. The noise roused Angel. Dirty Bob was frozen stiff with fear when she went to investigate what she had heard.

Dirty Bob mumbled his words before Angel could ask him what he saw. *"I saw nothing, and I know nothing."*

Angel then pulled out one of her guns. *"I'm sorry, but I don't leave witnesses."*

Dirty Bob had to plead for his life. *"I am already homeless, and I have nothing. The least you can do is let me live."*

Angel didn't have a choice; he was simply in the wrong place at the wrong time. Angel then put two bullets through Dirty Bob's skull with one of her MAC-10s. When Baby Girl heard the shots, she went into the empty store to make sure everything was fine.

When she saw Dirty Bob dead on the floor with his eyes wide open, Baby Girl almost screamed in horror. *"What the hell? Where did he come from?"*

"He was hiding in the back room. I thought I told you to check out the back of the store." Angel said.

Baby Girl knew she checked the back of the store to make sure she wasn't second-guessing herself. She returned to the store's backroom and looked in the room's corner where there was a pile of cardboard boxes. Dim Bob was hiding there because it had shifted the boxes to the far side of the room. Angel and Baby Girl hopped in the car and drove to the gas station. Angel returned to the empty store and poured gasoline all over it. Baby Girl lit a match and threw it on the cardboard boxes. Angel and Baby Girl walked out of the store without looking back.

Angel and Baby Girl returned to the hotel and checked out. They were going to Red Lobster to get a meal before leaving St. Louis. When they were parking in the Red Lobster parking lot, they noticed a man who appeared to be Black, so they had to hasten to find out who this man was going into Red Lobster. He resembled the man they had just assassinated.

Angel had some instructions for Baby Girl. "This is how we are going to play this out when we get inside the restaurant. I'm going to drop my purse. I'm going to bend over right m front of him so he could get a peek at my fat ass."

Angel's plan went off without a hitch, just as she had hoped. She dropped her purse to ensure she didn't leave her lipstick on the floor, allowing him to bring it to their table as planned. However, it surprised Angel and Baby Girl when Black's twin brother Smokey appeared at the table: they were identical. Angel invited him to lunch with her and Baby Girl to find out more information.

Smokey approached Angel, *"Hold up a minute, ma. I have a guest coming to join me. Is it all right if we all join you at your table?"*

Angel said, *"If it's all right with my sister, it's all right with me."*

Baby Girl knew what Angel was talking about, so she followed her suit. *"Sure, it's fine. Go get your crew so we can put our order in."*

Smokey came back to the table with three of his soldiers. He was sitting beside Angel, fantasizing about getting a room and clamming between Angel's legs.

Angel's thoughts were elsewhere. She was just hoping she hadn't killed the wrong guy, but she didn't care because killing was her job, and mistakes didn't exist in her business. They introduced themselves once everyone had returned to Angel's table. Angel introduced herself as Nicole, and Baby Girl introduced herself as Penny.

Smokey introduced himself. *"My name is Black. I have a twin brother, Smokey. We just switched places for the day to send the police in a different direction."*

Then Black introduced Angel to his three soldiers as Blocker, Hot Head, and Cricket. *"Nice to meet you,"* Angel and Baby Girl said in unison before excusing themselves for a bathroom break.

When Angel and Baby Girl went to the bathroom, they devised a plan to get another hotel room and bring their company with them. Angel noticed how Black kept staring at her behind and knew she could persuade him to accompany her to the hotel.

After finishing their meals, Black couldn't help but ask Angel, *"What are you about to get into?"*

"You know how black folks are after they eat. They be ready to go to sleep, so that's what I'm getting ready to do. I'm getting me a room and get some sleep for a couple of hours." Angel was about to stand up and leave.

Black had other plans. He wanted to follow Angel to her hotel. *"I hear you, ma. I just wish I could keep you company while you sleep, that's all."*

Angel almost hesitated, *"Well, let me get my room first. Maybe I might let you keep me company for a little while."*

Angel knew she was going to contact Black because they had not completed her mission to kill him. So, when she and Baby Girl arrived at the hotel, the front desk assigned two adjacent rooms to them. However, black was not going alone. He asked Angel if he could bring Cricket with him because there were two of them. Angel agreed as if she didn't mind at all. Cricket would not be a problem for her. He was five feet two inches tall and weighed one hundred pounds. She knew well that Baby Girl could easily break his neck.

Angel and Baby Girl drove to the Pear Tree Hotel. They made their reservations over the phone. Angel had piano string ready with a forty-four that she called Pistol Pete. She made sure that Baby Girl had her weapon of choice, too. Baby Girl requested the number forty-five. Angel had kept it in the car's glove compartment, so she went to get it. Baby Girl also wanted the two switchblades.

They remained in the room for two hours before calling Black and Cricket to come to their room. Angel ordered wine from room service and spiked it with enough LSD to knock them out cold. Black knocked on the door. He'd changed his clothes, and Angel told herself, *It doesn't even matter because this nigger here won't make it out of this room alive.*

Angel and Baby Girl had music playing in both rooms and two bottles of wine set aside for themselves so they wouldn't drink the spiked bottle. Black and Cricket were in a good mood when they came to a halt. They wished to perform a slow dance with Angel and Baby Girl. Angel grabbed Black's hand, yanked him off the bed, and began dancing. Baby Girl followed suit once more. When they looked up, Black's and Cricket's stupid assess were sleeping, standing up on their shoulders. The deadweight of the two men was about to knock them to the ground.

Angel looked at her daughter. *"You know what time it is?"*

Baby Girl told her mother, *"I have mine."*

Baby Girl grabbed Cricket's neck and snapped it before Angel could turn her head. He was dead, his body as limp as a dishrag. Angel left Black lying on the floor. She wrapped her piano wire around his neck and began pulling, but Black wasn't yielding as quickly as Cricket. He was fighting

Angel. Baby Girl crept up behind Black with her switchblade and slashed his throat from ear to ear; he slid down from Angel's leg to the floor, dead.

Angel and Baby Girl packed their shit, checked out the hotel, and returned to California. On their way out of the room, they wiped their fingerprints off everything in the room, including the doorknob. Angel and Baby Girl arrived home just in time for an envelope to be delivered to Angel's home. She had another assignment the following day, so she opened the envelope to see who her next target was, and she thought, *Damn, I thought I was done with Chicago.* Still, the Columbians had put a hit out on Mrs. Helen, her dead sister Isabella's mother.

Mrs. Helen was the Columbians' link to family services; she assisted them in placing some of their people in the United States, getting passports, and preventing immigration from discovering that they were sending people through the system under assumed names.

Helen decided she was sick of taking chances by assisting the Columbians. She nearly got caught twice on the job, and they weren't paying her enough to keep her job for twelve years. Mrs. Helen didn't realize that her death was being recorded and that she would see her daughter Isabella sooner than she expected because Angel was on her way back to Chicago, ready to put Mrs. Helen out of her misery. Angel drove straight to Mrs. Helen's house when she arrived in Chicago. Angel knew it was the same house because she passed by it when she got out of jail, but Angel couldn't bring herself to apologize to Mrs. Helen for her daughter's death. She demanded that Mrs. Helen pay for her father Cane's infidelity while her parents were still married.

Angel knew deep inside that she would kill Helen as soon as possible because she didn't want to waste any more of her time in Chicago until it was time for her to return to her position. She still had a lot of property in Chicago, and she wanted to keep everything she owned up there under her dummy corporation.

Angel smashed Helen's back door window and waited for Mrs. Helen to return home. Then Mrs. Helen walked straight to her recliner when she opened her front door. She'd do it every day when she got home because her feet hurt so much.

Mrs. Helen sat down, leaned back against the back of her recliner, closed her eyes, and took a deep breath. When she opened her eyes, it was too late; Angel wrapped an existing around her neck so tightly that her eyeballs nearly bulged out of her head. Mrs. Helen did not know that was the last breath she would take. Angel exited Mrs. Helen's home via the back door. She got back on the road and drove back to California, having completed another job.

Twenty-Six

～

Car Accident

Angel was driving back from Chicago when she felt dizzy. She attempted to keep her gaze fixed on the road. The highway was icy, and she couldn't pull over because it was clogged with people leaving work. Angel attempted to swerve her car onto the highway's right shoulder when hit by a large truck. Her vehicle was bent like a Pepsi can. Angel was knocked out cold. Angel was lying on the pavement when the ambulance arrived at the scene of the accident. The truck driver yanked her out of the car just as it exploded.

Angel was unconscious for five days. Baby Girl was frightened when she continued dialing Angel's phone and hearing voice mail. Angel had been away for five days, and Baby Girl was worried for her mother. Ramon assured Baby Girl that he would arrive before dark.

Ramon arrived at Angel's house on time and looked at Baby Girl. She was extremely pale. Baby Girl had gotten no good sleep in five days. *"Why didn't you call me days ago?"* he inquired.

"Because I didn't want to raise any red flags, I was hoping my mother had called by now. Something isn't right. I can sense it." Baby Girl started crying.

"Calm down, Baby Girl. I'll check the hospitals to see if there are any Jane Does." Ramon said.

Ramon dialed three hospitals before locating Angel. She'd been admitted to Mercy Hospital outside of Chicago as Jane Doe.

When Ramon and Baby Girl arrived at the hospital, she was still unconscious. Baby Girl looked at her mother and burst out crying because Angel didn't look like herself. Her face had swollen to the size of a beach ball. Ramon gave Angel's information to the hospital nurse to know who she was, and he insisted on round-the-clock care from all staff, no matter the cost.

Ramon and Baby Girl stayed with Angel at the hospital the entire time. She did not know they were there, but it didn't matter because they weren't leaving her side. Five days had passed, but Angel remained unconscious. Angel's vitals were checked by the doctor daily.

When Angel awoke, Ramon and Baby Girl were sleeping in a chair in her room. Her mouth was so dry that she couldn't speak. Angel called Baby Girl. Baby Girl was awakened by her mother's coughing, so she jumped to her feet and dashed over to Angel's bedside. She hugged and kissed her.

"Mommy, I thought you would not wake up. I've been praying for you to wake up." Baby Girl said.

Angel stared at Baby Girl, not realizing she was in the hospital until Ramon approached her bed. When Ramon bent down to kiss Angel, she realized she'd been in a car accident on her way home.

Angel suffered a shattered pelvis and had to be operated on. Her skull was broken, hence her prolonged unconsciousness. Her face and head swelled. She remembered her face collapsing against the steering wheel.

Angel spent three weeks in the hospital. After that, she wanted to return to work, but Ramon said she needed time to heal. Angel agreed, but required some outpatient therapy, so Ramon hired a hospital nurse to stay with her.

Angel got home after nearly a month in the hospital. Ramon stayed with Angel until she recovered, lavishing her with attention. She was spoiled rotten. Angel was quickly back on track. She was eager to return to work, but Ramon wanted her fully recovered first. So Ramon took Angel and Baby Girl back to Columbia to make sure she healed adequately.

Angel and Baby Girl had spent three weeks in Columbia. Ramon could tell Angel had healed because they were having rabbit sex. Angel notified Baby Girl it was time for them to return home.

"Are you sure? Because I'm having a great time." Baby Girl asked.

"Baby Girl, it's time. We have jobs, remember?" Angel stated.

Baby Girl eventually agreed, and Ramon flew them back home. That night, Angel and Baby Girl arrived home.

Angel was waiting for some college letters she had completed to prepare for Baby Girl's college enrollment. She had three acceptance letters from colleges she wanted her daughter to attend. Baby Girl desired to attend Spelman, which she was accepted. Baby Girl would leave in two weeks to attend Spelman.

Gloria dreaded leaving her mother. Even though they were both trained assassins, she worried about her mother's safety. Angel wanted Baby Girl to continue her schooling. She had more than a high school diploma in the parable. Gloria, aka Baby Girl, was heading to Spelman to become a lawyer.

Are you sure you want a degree in that? We're hired, killers. Angel asked.

"Yes, I'm sure, Mother. Because one day we might need someone on the inside to help us get out of a sticky situation." Baby Girl replied.

Angel wanted Baby Girl to get a real estate license because they had a lot of property on hold under a dummy corporation. Still, Angel plans to get her a real estate license under an assumed name while Baby Girl is at Spelman. Angel and Baby Girl went shopping for Baby Girl's school supplies and other dorm room necessities. They were gone for most of the day. When they got home, another envelope was slid under Angel's front door.

Angel didn't want Baby Girl to see the envelope because she wanted her to focus on college, but Baby Girl scooped it up from the floor before Angel could take it up. Baby Girl ripped open the envelope to reveal their next target: two African brothers named Barras and Baas.

Angel told her daughter she would work alone on the project because Baby Girl would leave for college in two weeks.

"Come on, Mom, another for the road."

"No, Baby Girl, no," Angel said.

Baby Girl's hands tasted like blood. It gave her a rush; she felt strong and unstoppable. Angel looked her daughter in the eyes and saw the killing instinct. She's more capable of being an assassin.

Angel studied her targets late that night. She was curious about them. The two brothers ran a drug ring in Cleveland, Ohio. But, unfortunately, they were too busy adorning themselves and getting high on the product that they didn't consider the consequences of messing up with the Columbians.

Angel knew where the African brothers hung out, and she also had their South Side Cleveland loft address. They indulged in sexual acts, prostitution, and orgies.

The brothers established Queen Bees, a brothel where prostitutes from all over came to take part in their sexual activities.

Angel thought. Those fools made a colossal mistake going up against the Columbians. Their brothel with female prostitutes will be my way in to get close to them.

Angel went to Victoria's Secret to get some nice and nefarious lingerie. She desired for the brothers' minds to be completely messed up.

Angel had a week to prepare her belongings for the trip to Cleveland. She had hoped to accompany her Baby Girl to college first, but time was not on her side. So instead, she'd have to go to Cleveland first, hit her goals, and then go to Spelman to make sure her Baby Girl was at ease in her new surroundings.

Angel was packing her arsenal to take to Cleveland when the idea of taking her Baby Girl to a car dealership struck her. Baby Girl did not know her mother would buy her the car of her dreams. Instead, she wished for a baby blue 2011 Mustang convertible.

Angel made a four-day reservation at the Hilton Garden Inn in Cleveland while they were at the car lot.

Thanks to Angel, baby Girl was thrilled to be driving off the lot in a brand-new convertible straight from the showroom floor. Angel was equally ecstatic. They had breakfast the following day before Angel left for Cleveland. Baby Girl kissed her mother goodbye and wished Angel a safe journey to Cleveland.

Baby Girl had her own plans. She studied her mother's target while Angel slept. She wouldn't leave her mother alone, knowing what she would be facing. After registering and receiving her assignments at Spelman, Baby Girl followed her mother. She called the hotel her mother was in and booked a room on a different floor. Baby Girl made sure she wouldn't get spotted by her mother. She was going to keep a close eye on her back. Whether she wanted her to, it's what she was trained to do.

Angel arrived at the Hilton hotel that morning and rented a Chrysler 300 with GPS. That was one item she didn't have to order as part of her rental. Angel arrived at the brothel just in time. All she had to do was walk in and introduce herself. Angel wanted the brothers to see what she was up to so they could compete for her attention because the other females in their brothel were pale compared to Angel. She was aware of it, as were they.

Glow stood outside the brothel, looking in. She rented a black Honda Accord from a car rental company. She didn't want to come across as suspicious. She intended to notify her mother that she had arrived unexpectedly, but that would have to wait until later. Angel put on a show later that night. She walked in Queen Bees wearing a black fur coat with nothing but a red bra set and red thigh-high stockings with red garters. She was also wearing six-inch red pumps.

Glow was sitting across the street when she saw her mother enter the brothel. She had a feeling something was about to happen. Glow was hypervigilant. She knew her mother too well. Glow thought to herself, "I need a disguise." She looked for a store where she could change her appearance. She needed a wig and contacts. She wanted to look older.

Angel was at the brothel's bar, sipping an apple martini, when Barras approached her and introduced himself. Angel was perplexed by his accent. She thought he sounded as country as hell. She worked hard not to laugh in his face. "Oh, I apologize. Candy is my name." Angel said, looking up into Baras' face.

"*Of course, your name is Candy because you look as sweet as hell,*" he said to Angel.

"*Is that right?*" Angel responded to Barras's remark.

"*That's right. How about you come over to my place and join me for some more apple martinis?*"

Angel agreed. She was curious about the layout of their loft, anyway. But, she thought to herself, typical man, they always think with their little heads. Their dicks are always their undoing because they want what they want when they want it.

Barras stood up, took Angel's hand, and they left the brothel for Barras' loft.

Baby Girl had just returned to the brothel when she noticed her mother exiting with Barras. He was giddy, as if he'd been given a free ticket to a baseball game. Angel did not know the brothers knew more about the Columbians than she did. They knew her coming from a mile away as she sat in the brothel getting her drink on. The brothers intended to kidnap and murder Angel.

Barras thought to himself. If she comes willingly with me, the kidnapping would be simple. When he saw Angel would go with him voluntarily, he knew she was up to something. While Barras and Angel were en route to the loft, Barras's brother Baas was already there, waiting for them. Angel was wearing a fur coat with two snug nose thirty-eights sewed inside, and they would never figure it out.

Barras was supposed to bring Angel to their loft and feed her cocaine-laced martinis. Instead, as soon as Angel walked in the front door, she asked to use the restroom. "Sure, the bathroom is down the hall to your right," Barras replied.

Baas emerged from the den holding a pair of handcuffs as soon as Angel closed the bathroom door. As soon as that bitch opens the bathroom door, you punch her in the face hard enough to knock her out. All right, Barras said,

"I got this. Go back into the den. I will bring her back there once I knock her out." Barras said.

Baas said okay and disappeared back down the hall.

Angel opened the bathroom door to come out. As Angel walked out the door, Barras smacked Angel in the face and Angel collapsed on the floor and passed out. When she awoke, she found herself handcuffed in Barras' bed. The brothers intended to rape Angel first, before killing her.

Baas was determined to be the first to rape Angel. She was the type of woman he liked, a redbone woman. He preferred women who were light and bright. Something about a fair-skinned woman gave his dick a hard-on. Barras got angry with his brother because he was the one who brought Angel and thus deserved to be the first to rape her.

Baas crawled up Angel's body, ready to attack, like a python in rear form. Then he began licking Angel's entire body. When his tongue arrived at Angel's honey pot, Baas dipped it so profoundly that Angel let out a loud sound of pleasure. He hadn't counted on it. That sped up his licking because she turned him on like a fire hose on a fire truck.

Barras was enraged as he watched his brother give Angel satisfaction. He wanted to be the one to light Angel's honey pot on fire.

Barras snatched his brother away from Angel and said, *"That's enough. It's my turn now."*

Standing there watching his brother do, Angel had given Barras a hard-on. He climbed on top of Angel and yanked his penis out, driving it hard into Angel's honey pot. "Hurry and bust your nut because I want some of that fat ass she got," his brother said.

Barras had finished busting his nut in Angel's, so he sat on the edge of the bed and watched his brother screw Angel in the ass. Angel was so high on cocaine from the brothel that she enjoyed what the two brothers were doing to her sexually.

She did not know what they would do to her next. They intended to beat Angel to death with their bare hands. What they didn't realize was that they were about to experience the element of surprise.

Baby Girl slammed the door off its hinges and stormed in, furious. Baby Girl knew something was wrong. Her mother was never on a set for more than an hour. She'd been inside the loft for almost two hours, which triggered a lousy signal alert in her brain. She carried two silencer-equipped forty-fives with pearl handles. When the brothers heard their door slam, they didn't grab their weapons because they thought it was Johnny law coming to arrest them.

Barras was the first to dash into the living room, his hand raised in the air. He would surrender without a fight, and his brother was right behind him. What they discovered was a huge mistake. Baby Girl shot them all over their bodies with her forty-fives, spewing bullets like a MAC-10. Both brothers collapsed to the ground like pincushions.

Baby Girl called out to her mother, but Angel couldn't respond because Baas had covered her up. He wrapped duct tape around her mouth to keep her from screaming. When Baby Girl opened the door to the bedroom, she discovered a blood-splattered blanket on the bed. She was terrified because she didn't want to find her mother dead beneath that blanket.

When Baby Girl moved the blanket, her mother was covered in blood from head to toe, but she was still alive. She'd been raped, and her nose had been broken. Baby Girl was so angry. She put her mother's coat on and escorted her out of the house, then she returned to the brothers' loft after Angel was in the car and emptied her guns on both of their faces.

Gloria returned to the Hilton, checked her mother in, and returned the rental car to Enterprise. She then returned to California with her mother. Angel was so out of it she couldn't recognize her own daughter.

On the way back to California, Baby Girl stopped at a hospital because her mother required immediate medical attention. Angel's nose was severely fractured. It had to be put back in place. The brothers had raped and drugged her. Baby Girl didn't want them to investigate her mother for rape. Still, she wanted them to do something about Angel's nose because she could hardly breathe.

Baby Girl didn't want to raise any suspicions about her mother being raped. She told the hospital that Angel was her sister, and they had been jumped by a gang of women at a club. The doctor who was examining Angel was also checking Baby Girl, so if she said the earth would blow up, he would have believed her. Dr. Mitchell asked Baby Girl to step out of the room while he and his nurse examined Angel. *"Okay, I'll be right outside the door,"* she said.

Dr. Mitchell asked Baby Girl to step back into the room after he finished examining Angel. He stated, "I know your sister was raped, and she has cocaine in her system. You know I am required to report my findings to the authorities."

Baby Girl sobbed, telling the doctor not to report what he discovered and that she and Angel would leave town as soon as he told her she was free to go. Dr. Mitchell told Baby Girl that if she had dinner with him and explained what really happened, he might reconsider calling the cops. Baby Girl went out to dinner with the doctor. Angel had a boyfriend in town who beat and raped her, and they weren't supposed to be in Cleveland at all.

Dr. Mitchell understood what Baby Girl told him and gave Angel the all-clear. The next day, Angel could go home with Baby Girl's condition to keep in touch with Dr. Mitchell about Angel's condition. She said fine, and Angel and Baby Girl drove back to California.

Angel healed and recovered sufficiently for Baby Girl to return to college. She left a week later to return to Spelman. Angel couldn't even get angry with her daughter for following her to Cleveland. She saved her life. Baby Girl would never have known what happened to her mother if she hadn't secretly followed Angel. Angel was heartbroken when her baby girl left for college. They talked on the phone every day.

Baby Girl even informed Angel that she had met a man named Raymond. She told Angel he was a cutie who went to a college near Spelman and majored in criminal justice. Angel warned Baby Girl not to look at anything differently while she was away from home. "Don't trust anyone."

Baby Girl said, *"Yes, Mother, I will be careful. I love you. I will call you next week."*

They said their goodbyes and hung up the phone.

Twenty-Seven

༺༅༎

Moving to Columbia

Uncle Leo called Angel and made an excellent proposition. Angel recognized Uncle Leo's voice when she answered the phone.

"Hello, Uncle Leo, so why do I have the honor of speaking to my favorite?" Angel answered.

She'd never had the pleasure of speaking with him on the phone. Uncle Leo would always send her envelopes with details, but when he called her himself, Angel knew it was personal.

"I want to propose something that you cannot refuse." Uncle Leo said.

Angel could sense the excitement in his Uncle Leo's voice and it piqued Angel's interest. *"Oh, you do? Okay, let's hear it if it's good. I might not. It depends on what it is."*

He desired Angel to consider moving to Columbia. He wanted her to run a high-priced escort service. Angel was a stunning, elegant, classy, and a wealthy woman. She stood out among the other women in the escort service. Uncle Leo put Angel in her own category.

Angel was more than happy to accept Uncle Leo's offer when he laid out the business to her. She'd have more money, and she'd still be able to go out on assignments once a month. So Angel has agreed to move to Columbia at the end of the month. Uncle Leo had his moving crew ready to travel to California and resettle Angel to Columbia.

Angel had set everything in motion to move to Columbia. She wanted to tell Baby Girl in person, so she drove down to Spelman to surprise her daughter, only to discover that Baby Girl had forgotten to tell her mother that they had kicked her out of Spelman for selling drugs on campus. Angel had a GPS tracking device installed on her daughter's phone before she left for Spelman, but Angel had utterly forgotten about it until she was at Spelman, standing there looking lost. The situation enraged Angel because they talked on the phone every day, and she didn't even mention it to her once.

Angel activated the tracking device, which led her to Raymond's dorm room. She couldn't believe what she saw. Baby Girl was smoking on a crack pipe made of glass. Angel tried to figure out what had happened in the last three weeks. She grabbed Baby Girl and dragged her out. She would put her daughter in rehab because she had become so thin as if Baby Girl hadn't eaten in weeks. Angel was desperate to see this Raymond character because he had strung her daughter out on crack cocaine. He should have been a dead man if Angel caught up with him; it just so happened that he was on a drug run when Angel showed up on them.

When Baby Girl told Angel about Raymond, she was lying the entire time. She didn't want Angel to know the truth about Raymond. Raymond was a drug lord.

Angel thought to herself; *I would have felt better if she told me he was a doctor or he was a street pharmacy.*

Angel had an epiphany. She thought it would be in her Baby Girl's best interest to take Raymond off the map. He was a thorn in Angel's throat. She didn't want her daughter traveling in the same circles as him. For her, Baby Girl is a true soldier.

Angel wasn't too upset with her daughter. She took Baby Girl straight to rehab with strict rules: no visitors, just her. Angel wanted her to kick her drug habit on her own. She wanted Baby Girl to avoid Raymond at all costs.

Angel returned home and packed her belongings to prepare for the

movers transporting her to Columbia. She had her things moved to Columbia first, and then she went back to the rehab and stayed with Baby
Girl.

Baby Girl was on suicide watch at the rehab facility 24 seven. She attempted suicide twice, covering her hands in blood. Angel was aware of
what was bothering her daughter. Maybe she taught her too young, or
perhaps she can't bear the thought of taking another person's life. Whatever the reason, this made Angel determined to get her daughter out of
the mess and back on track. But first, she had to deal with the idiot who
had sent her Baby Girl to rehab.

Angel returned to Spelman and requested to meet with the dean. Angel knew that money talk and bullshit worked. Baby Girl belonged at
Spelman, a prestigious and highly selective women's college, and Angel
wanted her back in. Angel talked to the dean for hours, and right after the
negotiation, they accepted her Baby Girl back with no problems.

Angel said a prayer. She said to herself, *I of all people praying, but this
is for my daughter, not me. I need your help, Lord, in watching over my
daughter.* After Angel left the dean's office, she made a detour to find this
Raymond guy. He had to pay the piper for getting her daughter hooked
on crack.

Angel returned to the dorm room where Raymond stays, but Raymond ran up to her car as if she were a junkie when she arrived. Angel
shot Raymond twice in the head. There was no one around to see her, so
Angel got away unscathed.

Two months later, the rehab authorities released Baby Girl, and Angel
drove her back to Spelman. She told Baby Girl they would stay in Columbia for some time. Baby Girl was happy that they could finally stay
in Columbia. She had a great time there, especially with Uncle Leo. The
Columbian mafia family adored Angel and her daughter.

Angel moved into the villa Uncle Leo bought for her. He had it all fur-
nished and set up as if she were a Columbian princess. She set up her com-
puters and logged into Facebook, Twitter, and e-mail. Angel intended to
run the escort service as if it were a legal business. She had at least twenty
exotic women under her supervision. Angel felt like she was a Columbian

madam, and that was exactly what she was. She worked twice a month as an assassin and for the rest of the year as a madam. Angel's plate was definitely full.

Twenty-Eight

◡◠

Columbian Madam

Angel had settled into her new villa. She renamed the villa Uncle Leo wants her to administer. Angel disliked the name Slice of Life, so she asked Uncle Leo whether she might alter the name to attract customers. "I want you to do whatever you think will make it popular," he told Angel. Angel had chosen a new name for it. She called it Sexy Ladies.

Angel and Ramon got really close when she moved to Columbia. They spent a lot of time together. Ramon treated her like his little princess. They went on dates, and Ramon even took Angel on a canoe picnic. Angel and Ramon had sex regularly. They got so toasted one night they had unprotected sex. She was sure she wouldn't conceive until after two months; she gained weight on her hips and breasts.

Uncle Leo hosted a dinner party to welcome Angel to Columbia. Angel tried on some of her clothes but couldn't fit into any of them. *"This isn't right,"* she thought to herself. *"This outfit fitted me two months ago,"* Angel remembered the night she and Ramon had sex without a condom. Shit! she exclaimed. My ass could be pregnant. Angel decided to see a doctor in town. She was still having her period, but her body felt different this time.

Angel went to the doctor. She had to wait because she had no appointment. Angel got up and went into the room where the nurse took her vitals. She then gave Angel a cup to collect urine for the lab before the doctor examined her. Angel was told to strip from the waist down so the doctor could examine her. The nurse said the doctor would be in shortly.

Angel waited for the doctor to arrive. But, unfortunately, she was engrossed with her thoughts that she didn't even notice the doctor knocking on the door before entering the room.

"Why do you want to see me today, and what are your concerns?" He inquired of Angel.

"I've been gaining weight and feeling sleepy all the time. I haven't missed my period, but my body is acting strangely." Angel explained to the doctor.

The doctor instructed Angel to lie back and scoot down to the end of the table so that he could examine her. When Angel did what the doctor told her to do, the nurse returned to the room with Angel's urine test results. Angel was indeed pregnant. When the doctor finished his examination, he explained why Angel's body felt so different. He informed Angel that she suffers from a condition known as preeclampsia, a disorder that occurs during pregnancy, and the postpartum period affects both the mother and the unborn child.

Dr. Bishop explained preeclampsia in greater detail, so Angel could better understand the condition. He explained to Angel that the symptoms of preeclampsia include swelling of the hands, face, and eyes and sudden weight gain. Pregnancy hypertension was also a complication of the condition.

"What is the treatment for preeclampsia?" Angel inquired of the doctor.

"There are a lot of different treatments for the condition, but it's also a high-risk pregnancy," he added.

Angel had a lot on her mind as she walked out of the doctor's office. She wasn't ready to tell Ramon about her condition. Instead, she simply wanted to absorb the situation a little more before telling him.

Angel returned to the villa and resumed her work. She pretended as if nothing was wrong with her. Uncle Leo hired her to do a job, so that's exactly what she would do.

Angel woke the girls up early one Friday morning. She made them get tested for venereal infections. It's one thing Angel made clear to them. Angel requested the doctor to provide her with all the test results, and she made sure they had enough supply of condoms. Teri was the one rotten apple among the girls. Angel did not appeal to her. For her, Angel was too young to be the establishment's madam.

Teri wished to speak with Uncle Leo about Angel. She didn't want any child telling her what she should do, and Teri had the impression she was old enough to be Angel's mother. So Teri went up to the villa to confront Uncle Leo about her dissatisfaction with the way Angel ran things.

"If you don't like what's going on, you can leave, but you can't take anything with you," Uncle Leo told Teri.

Teri was angry because she believed she was entitled to keep whatever she had since she brought in the most money.

"You better not start any trouble because if you do, I will hang you from a tree buck naked so the entire village can see you for the whore you really are," Uncle Leo warned Teri.

Angel knew Teri was going to be a headache. Teri was running the place down to the ground before Uncle Leo summoned her to take over. She was stealing money and letting the girls do whatever they wanted as the money came to her. Uncle Leo only kept her because he promised her father before killing him that Teri would never be homeless.

Angel went shopping with the girls to get them some proper, much-needed clothing because they were dressed like homeless hookers. She wanted them to look like lady callers of the night and not as they came from a hoe strolling down Chicago's streets. Angel wanted them to look like high-class, elegant, and glamorous women because that's who they were. She even did their make-up. Uncle Leo couldn't contain himself when Angel finished making over all the girls.

Teri was still a nuisance. She started scheming against Angel. She told the girls they were doing all the fucking, and Angel was benefiting. Teri also said Angel was fucking Uncle Leo.

"How did you think she got the job as madam? I don't think she came all the way from California to stay here. That young lady is Leo's personal assassin. She has now moved to Columbia to take over as madam. That's bullshit, and we all know it." Teri told the girls.

Angel was close to a few of the girls, and one girl mentioned the gossip of Teri's habit of sticking her foot in her mouth. Angel decided it was time to call Teri in her office and find out what was wrong with her. Angel hoped she didn't have to kick Teri in the shins to make her point, but she wasn't concerned. Let the chips fall where they may because this shit ends today. She told herself.

Teri strutted into Angel's office as if she was ready for battle. But, unfortunately, she did not know she was dealing with the right one because Angel wanted to stomp a hole in her ass as well. Angel motioned for Teri to take a seat, but she declined.

"All right, whatever, I called you in here today because I heard you didn't like the way I was running things," Angel said.

But before Angel could say another word, Teri said,

"I don't like the way you came all the way from California with your desire to be pretty ass trying to run things differently than I was running them."

"Oh, you angry because I stopped your little side hustle," Angel said to Teri.

"Look here, bitch, you didn't stop shit. Leo is fucking your stank ass. That's why he chose you to take my place because he would not get any more free pussy."

"If you call me a bitch just one more time, they'll be zipping your ass up in a plastic bag," Angel warned Teri.

Teri began clenching her fists tightly. *"If you feel threatened by me, jump or do your heart pump, Kool-Aid bitch,"* she told Angel.

Teri knew she didn't stand a chance with Angel. Like everyone else in Columbia, she knew Angel was a hired killer, so what she was trying to go up against her was beyond Angel. When Teri spit bitch out her mouth again, Angel jumped across her desk and smacked Teri in the jaw so hard that it broke on impact. Teri attempted to pull Angel's hair by grabbing her long ponytail.

No, bitch, you asked for an ass whipping, and I'm the right bitch to give you what you asked for, Angel said.

Angel and Teri were fighting so hard, so one girl ran up to the villa to get Uncle Leo and Ramon. They paused for a moment because they hadn't seen two women fight in a long time, and Angel hadn't told them yet she was pregnant. Teri looked like she'd been in a boxing ring with Sugar Ray Leonard for two rounds when Ramon and Leo separated them. She had been ripped apart, and both of her eyes were black.

I warned you what would happen if you started any trouble, Uncle Leo said to Teri.

Uncle Leo grabbed Teri by her hair and snatched her clothes off, and she was hung outside in a tree by Ramon. He beat Teri with a bullwhip until she passed out. Teri hung in the tree for three days before Leo put her down. After that, she returned to work in Sexy Ladies with Angel, saying nothing else. Teri acted as if her tongue had been severed from her mouth. She didn't speak to anyone for a month, and her body was in pain the entire time.

Twenty-Nine

༉

Angel and The Columbian Cartel

Uncle Leo had a problem. The Columbian cartel had overstepped their bounds and were on the verge of declaring war on Uncle Leo's territory. They were sending threats to the Columbian mafia, threatening to take over the West Side of Columbia, putting Uncle Leo and his crew no choice but to move or be pushed out. There was a lot of money to be made on the West Side, and they clarified that everyone on that set would be shut down. Unfortunately, the Columbian cartel tried to enter the wrong doors.

Uncle Leo won't go down like that. He had all of his soldiers ready for battle and his secret weapon was ready to go. Angel was prepared. She had mass-destructive weapons and was just waiting for Uncle Joe, Uncle Leo's eldest brother, to give her the green light. Angel was about to turn in for the night when Uncle Joe summoned her to their villa, so she dressed up in her ninja suit and walked out the door.

Uncle Joe desired the entire West Side be erased from the map, so he told Angel to set up C4s at the cartel's compound. Uncle Joe even paid military personnel to assassinate everyone in the Columbian cartel. Unfortunately, the cartel had more clout than Uncle Joe realized. They knew how they got down and dirty, and the cartel had an inside connection.

Teri was on both sides of the fence. She was retaliating for what Uncle Leo had done to her, and she also wanted Angel's ass kicked.

Uncle Leo claimed that someone in their camp had been trading secrets. He stated, *"The motherfuckers knew too much. If I find out who they are, they will die slowly and agonizingly. Right now, I want everyone to take a lie detector test." Wake everybody up. I will not rest until I find out who in my camp had the nerve to trade secrets with my fucking enemies.*

Angel thought to herself. *"That bitch Teri been awful quiet around here. I'll bet a million dollars that she's the culprit. If she is, I feel sorry for her because what Uncle Joe has planned for the trader is akin to pulling teeth with wire pliers."*

Everyone in the compound, including Angel, took a lie detector test. That's when they found out she was pregnant because she still had told no one until then.

Everyone passed the lie detector test except Teri. Uncle Joe got pissed. He told everyone that they could return to their villas. He told Teri, *You can stay. I need to talk to you about something important.*

Before Teri could say a thing to defend herself. Uncle Joe stated: *"Bitch, say nothing. Screaming is the only sound I'm going to hear from you. You made your bed, and you're going to sleep in it. I knew you'd be trouble the day my brother murdered your father, but he promised your father he'd take care of you. So you'll be dancing with your father in hell now."*

Uncle Joe, Uncle Leo, and Ramon took Teri to the gun house. They rigged her up to a high beam in the ceiling. She was yelling and sobbing uncontrollably. Uncle Joe told Teri, *you can scream as long as you want for now because that's the last sound we'll ever hear coming out of your mouth.*

Uncle Joe used a blowtorch to burn Teri's skin off her body. When he was finished burning Teri alive, he took some alcohol and slathered it all over her burned skin; you could smell Teri's flesh burning like a side of beef.

Teri's screams could be heard by everyone in their villas. Then, the screaming abruptly came to a halt. It was all over. Teri would eventually write a check that her ass couldn't cash, and the girls knew it. Angel was relieved Teri wasn't around to cause any more trouble because she was going to bust a couple of caps in Teri's ass herself.

Angel did as she was told and placed C4s around the Columbian cartel's compound. She had all the detonators set to blow up their compound.

After the Columbian mafia murdered Teri that night, everyone was sleeping too much. It had been silent until they heard a loud boom. It was a series of bombs detonated throughout the compound. The Columbian cartel had slipped in unnoticed, and they were destroying Uncle Leo's compound.

People were running outside with their bodies on fire. Luckily, Angel and Ramon made it to their safe house underground. But, unfortunately, everyone else, including their uncles, had died.

Angel and Ramon needed to find a way out of Columbia without being apprehended. Their lives were in jeopardy. The cartel was still on their tail until Angel remembered she had set up their camp to be blown up as well.

Angel detonated the detonators. In an instant, the cartel's facility erupted. But Angel wasn't able to kill everyone. The cartel's boss, Mr. Sanchez, was trapped in his car, but it blew up after his driver tried to ignite it. One of his soldiers held his son, trying to escape to save his father, but it was too late. Mr. Sanchez's car flew as if it was being carried away by a twister.

Mr. Sanchez's son, Marcos, demanded heads for his father's death. He knew who was responsible since Teri told him about Angel, the Columbian mafia assassin. He knew Angel and had her pictures. Marcos also knew that her daughter Gloria attended Spelman. That led him to go to the United States to find Angel's daughter and bring Angel out of hiding.

Marcos considered murdering either Angel or her daughter, but he was so enraged that he told himself, *They must both die. Because of that bitch, I've lost everything, and my entire family is dead, so she must pay with her life and the life of her child.*

Angel and Ramon fled Columbia. They slipped past the Columbian cops, boarded Ramon's helicopter, and flew back to California, where they stayed in a hotel under fake identities. They needed to find a place to live because Angel was expecting Ramon's first child. Ramon assured Angel that everything would be fine, but they both knew that he'd be looking for them as long as Marcos was alive.

Marcos made his way to California, but he did not know where to look for Angel. Also, he did not know where Angel stayed in California. Then, Marcos remembered Teri gave him a postcard from Angel's daughter that she had sent her from Spelman while Angel was in Columbia. He also had a photo of Gloria. Marcos thought Angel would emerge from under a rock to save her daughter if he kidnapped Gloria. Still, Marcos didn't realize that Angel's Baby Girl was also an assassin.

The following day, Marcos flew to Atlanta, Georgia. He hired a car and drove to Spelman. He was so upset that he didn't even bother checking into a hotel. Marcos demanded that Angel pay with her blood. They took his son and wife from him. His son was only two weeks old when Angel blew up their compound. Marcos wanted Angel's daughter to suffer the same fate as his wife and son.

Angel contacted Baby Girl at school to inform her of everything that happened. She instructed her daughter to keep an eye out for Marcos. She even sent Marcos photos so she could see how he looked. Baby Girl assured her mother that everything was under control. She even told Angel that she had all of her artillery ready and waiting if he showed up.

"Be careful, and I'll be there in a couple of days," Angel advised.

Angel and Ramon flew to Atlanta to be with Baby Girl, although she knew her daughter could handle herself. She just wanted to be there to watch her back.

Baby Girl saw Marcos outside the university, spying on her. She mentally noted the plates. Her mother was right because that same car followed her everywhere she went, so she remained vigilant. However, Baby Girl knew better than to get caught doing anything. It wasn't in the assassin's rule book.

Angel booked a room at the Ramada Inn. This time, she didn't want to stay in a high-priced hotel. Instead, she desired to stay in a location where Marcos would be. Angel had intended to follow him when he left Spelman. Instead, she and Baby Girl had devised a trap for him.

Ramon used his GPS to locate a costume shop. He knew exactly how to get Marcos to leave his square. But, of course, he wouldn't expect them to be disguised. Ramon and Angel dressed up as two elderly people. Baby Girl planned to disguise herself as Raphael, a drag queen. For this kill, the three of them were going way out on a limb. They desired Marcos as much as he wanted them. Angel asked her daughter to take Marcos to a hotel where they could wait in the room for him to arrive. However, Angel knew he wouldn't follow her daughter voluntarily, so she had to force his hand.

Marcos saw Gloria enter the Holiday Inn, but he didn't know which room she went into, so he paid the front desk clerk $200 to give him the room number and the key. He explained to the clerk that they were married. It was their anniversary, and he wanted to surprise his wife. The clerk gave Marcos the room number and the master key to the room.

Marcos reached the third floor and saw room 333. He slid the master key in the door. He heard the shower running upon entering the room, so he thought he had the upper hand on Gloria. However, when Marcos entered the bathroom with his weapon drawn, he was hit in the back with an ashtray. He was knocked out.

When Marco awoke, he was tied to a chair and suffering from a severe headache. His head was swollen, and blood was dripping down his face. When he opened his eyes, he saw Angel. He began kicking to break free. He despised Angel and wished to kill her with his bare hands.

Ramon had three silencer-equipped forty-fives. He gave one to Baby Girl and one to Angel. They all took a step back, looked at Marcos, and laughed. Then, they all fired and emptied their weapons at Marcos, and when his head dropped, they thought it was over, and he'd never come after them again. Angel, Ramon, and Baby Girl didn't realize that the Columbian cartel was a vast organization. Mr. Sanchez's brother, Josh, has four sons who will hunt them down with a vengeance.

Angel took Baby Girl back to Spelman. She also informed her she was three months pregnant and would have a brother or a sister in six months.

Baby Girl was giddy with delight. She always wanted a sibling to whom she could pass on her expertise. So Angel and Ramon moved to California for good. They purchased a ranch-style home and decorated the nursery for their new family member.

Angel and Ramon discovered that Uncle Joe and Uncle Leo had fled from the compound underground a year later. They escaped through the tunnel beneath Uncle Joe's bedroom. They decided not to contact them until it was safe to do so, and after the case was resolved and the mafia was reassembled.

Angel took care of her preeclampsia and had to stay in bed for the last two months of her pregnancy to rest. Her two months were quickly approaching, so she decided to have an ultrasound to find out her actual due.

Angel's water broke while she was in the shower, getting ready for her ultrasound appointment. She was about to have her baby on the day she was scheduled for an ultrasound. Angel was in full-fledged labor, so Ramon rushed her to the hospital.

Angel was in labor for an hour before giving birth to a seven-pound, eight-ounce, twenty-one-inch boy. Ramon was giddy with delight. While Ramon was admiring his new son, Uncle Joe called. He informed Ramon that the mafia family had retaken control and that he and Angel needed to return to Columbia. Ramon told his uncle that Angel had recently given birth and that now would not be a good time. It would take at least six weeks before Angel could do anything, but they would keep in touch.

Uncle Joe said, *"Sure, you guys enjoy with your son. I will be in touch. Tell Angel that we all love her and that her job is still waiting for her."*

Angel was eager to return to work as a Columbian assassin. All she needed was to lose the baby weight. She'd be right back on top of her game once she did that. Her life had been a series of twists and turns. She cannot stop now.

Angel, the Columbian assassin—the saga continues!

CPSIA information can be obtained
at www.ICGtesting.com
Printed in the USA
LVHW091447220122
708554LV00006B/6